D0777037

MALE

THE "FRENCH WRITERS OF CANADA" SERIES

The purpose of this series is to bring to English readers, for the first time, in a uniform and inexpensive format, a selection of outstanding and representative works of fiction by French authors in Canada. Individual titles in the series will range from the most modern work to the classic. Our editors have examined the entire repertory of French fiction in this country to ensure that each book that is selected will reflect important literary and social trends, in addition to having evident aesthetic value.

Current titles in the Series

Ethel and the Terrorist, a novel by Claude Jasmin, translated by David Walker.
The Temple on the River, a novel by Jacques Hébert, translated by Gerald Taaffe.
Ashini, a novel by Yves Thériault, translated by Gwendolyn Moore.
N'Tsuk, a novel by Yves Thériault, translated by Gwendolyn Moore.
The Torrent, novellas and short stories by Anne Hébert, translated by Gwendolyn Moore.
Dr. Cotnoir, a novel by Jacques Ferron, translated by Pierre Cloutier.
Fanny, a novel by Louis Dantin, translated by Raymond Chamberlain.
The Saint Elias, a novel by Jacques Ferron, translated by Pierre Cloutier.

(Continued inside back cover)

Jacques Ferron

"Just who is Jacques Ferron?" this question was posed very pertinently by John Grube in a recent review of *The Saint Elias* in *Books in Canada*. His answer deserves to be given here in full.

"First of all he is more or less the 'Godfather' of Quebec literature, keeping a paternal eye on the careers of troublesome young Quebec writers, understanding their problems and occasionally smoothing their way. This can only be done by someone who quite literally knows everyone who matters in Quebec well, who is by birth and professional standing a 'notable,' who understands better than anyone else his people's history, and who is, finally, prepared to give that history a powerful imaginative projection in his own literary work. Not that he would ever take himself that seriously. Quite the contrary. His conversation, his correspondence, his novels, his celebrated letters to *Le Devoir* are full of the most delightful and self-deprecating irony. And yet he

really was there at the beginning of the Automa-
tiste movement in the 1940's, and in *Le Ciel de
Québec* gives an excruciatingly sensitive account
of Borduas' artistic agonies, and of Claude
Gauvreau's in *Du fond de mon arrière-cuisine*.
He really was the only person Trudeau and Paul
Rose could agree on to arrange the peaceful sur-
render of the FLQ's Chénier cell in December,
1970, and that was only possible because he knew
personally and understood both men. And he
really is the only person ever to have received the
praise of the conservative Catholic head of the St.
Jean-Baptiste Society, and of the revolutionary
Vallières of *Les nègres blancs d'Amérique*. The
point is that you cannot separate the medical
doctor, the writer, the mischievous practical
joker, the tough-minded Quebec politician, the
family man and the journalist without misunder-
standing the real Jacques Ferron. They are the
same integrated and perfectly delightful person.
That is why good translations are so much more
important than doctoral dissertations.''

THE
SAINT ELIAS

by
JACQUES FERRON

translated by
Pierre Cloutier

Advisory Editors

Ben-Zion Shek,
Department of French,
University of Toronto.

Réjean Robidoux,
Département d'Études Françaises,
University of Ottawa.

ISBN 88772 147 8
Deposited in the Bibliothèque Nationale of
Quebec
1st quarter, 1975.
Originally published in the French language
by Les Éditions du Jour, Montreal,
as *Le Saint-Élias*.

For information, address Harvest House Ltd.
4795 St. Catherine St. W., Montreal,
Quebec H3Z 2B9

Printed and bound in Canada.

Designed by Robert Reid.
Cover illustration: ''View of the Harbour,
Montreal, 1830'', by R.H. Sproule,
McCord Museum, Montreal

The Publishers gratefully acknowledge a
translation and publication grant from The
Canada Council.

for Clément Marchand

Glory and beauty endure, Kamalouk. As you are aware that they have existed, know that they shall return.

Marius Barbeau

CHAPTER 1

Between seed-time and hay-making, on the occasion of a great gathering at which the neighbors from Sainte-Anne-de-la-Pérade and Champlain were noticeably absent, a three-master was launched in Batiscan. It was destined to travel beyond the Straits of Newfoundland and reach Bermuda and the West Indies. Some even said that if need be, it could sail to the old country and return manned by an exclusively Batiscanese crew. The ship was christened *The Saint Elias*. His Excellency, Bishop Charles-Olivier Caron, Apostolic Protonotary and chaplain of the Ursulines, had come down from Trois-Rivières. He had previously headed two seminaries, by turns, acting as successor to the illustrious Father Ferland in one of them. And, although he had once taken precedence over His Excellency Bishop Laflèche, he was now the latter's subordinate, however indispensable he remained to the diocese under his immediate jurisdiction. The use of such power had made him versatile, so that he could be at once amiable and sly without getting into personal difficulties. He was respected all the more for this quality and thoroughly enjoyed the regard in which he was held. He spoke first and, without seeming to, introduced the speech of Father Elias

Tourigny, the local parish priest who wasn't much of an orator and who, to everyone's surprise, was miraculously eloquent for once. After the christening and the launching of the ship, it was his turn to speak. He then spoke words which were already on the lips of everyone present. This at first seemed merely astonishing, then prodigious, and finally gave rise to enthusiastic shouting.

Bishop Caron had begun with the words: "Just who are you people of Batiscan?" He seemed surprised to be asking such a question since he came from the same diocese, and was himself a native of Rivière-du-Loup, upstream from Trois-Rivières, between Machiche and Maskinongé.

"God has laden me with titles and honors, but never mind the frills, I'm still the boy I was and that boy didn't have golden buckles on his shoes. He went barefoot. In front of his parents' farm, a river which had as much water as yours and perhaps more, flowed by slowly. The only fleet you could ever see there was made up of fishing boats and one had to row to travel downstream. It emptied itself into Lac St. Pierre, a lake which drowns out the St. Lawrence because of its sheer size and from the river's mouth we couldn't even catch sight of the south shore and the two steeples of Baie-du-Fèvre. There was water and more water drifting among the reeds, the arrowheads and the water lilies. The lake was as large as it was shallow and the St. Lawrence was drowned in three, five, at the most ten feet of water. You might say it was resting and persuading the river-side parishes not to sail the high seas.

I really wonder why I should be talking to you at all on this great day. I feel I am nothing but a fisherman myself. I feel as if I have given in to the fake laziness of our river, to Lac St. Pierre. Out at Pointe-du-Lac, it falls back into line and goes flowing on, taking a right view of things. From my room in the Ursuline monastery I can catch sight of the Sainte-Angèle pier. Standing here, I feel as if I were on the steps of Saint-Pierre-les-Becquets church. After a carefree childhood I might not wish to follow the straight and narrow path of the Gospel. Still this is the way it is. The swift river, flowing right by between Sainte-Angèle and Trois-Rivières, this waterway into which the Batiscan flows, travelling along towards the Gulf and the open sea, is the truth. I come from a land of illusion and the Lord set me free in the bounty of his grace. The Batiscan doesn't come to an end in reeds and water lilies. It is a road leading to a bigger highway still. It makes you see things as they are. Facing facts makes you brave. This marvellous ship certainly holds more tonnage than the old rowboat I used to own in Rivière-du-Loup. And I'm still standing barefoot in that boat when I ask you: just who are you people?''

Father Tourigny was scheduled to speak after Bishop Charles-Olivier Caron. Everyone had noticed that His Excellency had been breaking the ice, yet Canon Elias Tourigny's speech wasn't expected to amount to much. He was a good priest but didn't know a thing about public speaking. What's more, he loved horses — had the best horse and buggy in the parish — and didn't care for the river at all. All he liked about it was the ice-bridge which allowed him to go places and do things with the folks back home in Saint-Pierre-les-Becquets, and some wondered whether the ship should have been christened *The Saint Elias* in his honor after all. Standing in front of a group of dignitaries, immediately behind the clergy,

11

you could see Doctor Fauteux who didn't much care for ecclesiastics and never went to church.

"There's no one from Champlain or La Pérade present," said Father Tourigny. "It seems they were celebrating Corpus Christi a week in advance. They're in a hurry and more power to them, but I hope the churchwardens won't take a spill rushing about with the dais."

The crowd burst out laughing and then glanced at Bishop Caron who laughed boisterously himself, so that everyone felt reassured.

"I would regret their absence if His Excellency Bishop Laflèche hadn't sent his most eminent representative to find out just who we are. I wouldn't venture to say, as he has, that a fisherman can't know what going out to sea means. Just think of the apostles who were fishermen. Think of the Lake of Tiberias which was only a kind of Lac St. Pierre but also happens to have been the scene of countless wonders. What we appreciate most in the presence of the delegate of His Excellency, is not so much the rowboat of his boyhood as that he is the outstanding scholar of the diocese, the man who journeyed to Rome and who headed seminaries in Nicolet and Trois-Rivières by turns. Under the circumstances, I hope he may understand what we're trying to achieve here and realize what kind of people we are."

Dr. Fauteux gave the cue for vigorous applause, showing his fondness the first time ever for Holy Mother Church, or at least his liking for the priest, who, from then on, had to stretch out his sentences so as not to be cheered continually. Father Armour Lupien, the curate, who was rather keen on rhetoric, couldn't understand what was going on, since the pastor had never sounded like much of an orator to

12

him. He wondered whether the Holy Spirit had descended on Father Tourigny, although he hadn't been dealing in divinity, mentioning only a river, a town and a people.

"When the French pulled out, we were pent up in this region. We had to pin our faith on our own capacity to survive. There was no other way of making it. A people which isn't self-reliant loses faith, loses its soul. We were captives, which means we couldn't get out. Granted we didn't have much of a navy but nothing kept us from building ships except that we'd bolted the door shut ourselves. Right after the Conquest, we began to tell each other cock-and-bull stories, each more hair-raising than the next about ships piloted by *Canadiens* getting wrecked out in the Gulf. The first of these legends dates back to Father Crespel. Now, if he had gone aboard one of the ships heading for France and piloted by Frenchmen you'd never have heard about this pious Capuchin friar. The one he boarded had a *Canadien* at the helm and went no farther than Anticosti. Father Crespel was one of the few who survived the shipwreck. It occurred during the fall, and he went through plenty of pain and suffering, so much so that he wrote a book about it, a few copies of which found their way to these shores; some were even transcribed by hand. Above all, the tale of the shipwreck was told high and low in Quebec and people said, over and over again, that the French ships had sailed on without being disabled; the moral of the story being that outsiders could come and go at will while we couldn't leave our country. Besides, why would we do it? Where could we have gone? Where were we expected? Nowhere, obviously. In fact, the whole thing became a convenient alibi which helped us feel good and snug in a place we didn't really care to leave. This disaster…''

''All the same, he does know a lot about the country,'' thought Father Lupien,'' and he has considered what he was going to say.''

''This disaster,'' Father Tourigny went on, ''was followed by several others, accounts of which were bandied about far and wide. The colleague of a friend I have seldom seen attending church services, the good Dr. Larue, chipped in recently with all his well-known liveliness. This time, instead of mentioning Anticosti, he chose the Newfoundland coast, bearing in mind that season of shipwrecks *par excellence,* the fall, with its ice floes and its agony. As Father Surprenant said to the eminent doctor:

''I don't care whether it happened near Anticosti or Newfoundland, but you should know that your eloquence is keeping us cooped up here.''

''I can see him coming,'' thought Father Lupien.

''Your Excellency would like to know who we are. Well, as to millet, oats, horses and cattle, I'm afraid I may disappoint you. We are like the older parishes west of the Saint-Maurice, those of Machiche, Rivière-du-Loup and Maskinongé.''

What happened then was unheard of. Bishop Caron stood up, interrupting the speaker.

''Well, don't come and tell me you've just been launching a cow, Father.''

The ship hadn't stabilized and the masts and spars showed that it was still rocking. Down-river, one could see the mouth of the Batiscan opening out on the St. Lawrence and the church of Saint-Pierre-les-Becquets standing on the south shore.

Father Tourigny didn't budge. He let Bishop

Laflèche's delegate sit down and answered:

"Your Excellency, I wouldn't want to denigrate the catfish and perch of which a boy was proud when they lay on the bottom of his rowboat and I have lived and let live, perhaps at the expense of our self-respect, but I will say we're not talking about catfish and beef on the hoof here. Besides being what you are, we're sailors and we have a fleet made up of bigger things than your small craft, if I may say so. It used to be roughly the size of Champlain's or La Pérade's, but it's something else again thanks to this three-master you see floating on the river."

Father Tourigny gave a detailed description of the ship.

"You may wonder why we built it, and I'll tell you why. We wanted to be free. Being confined here may have been good enough at a time when we weren't a people. Well, we have become a people now. Let the Gulf release us! Let the inhibitions of childhood come to an end! We built *The Saint Elias* to put out to sea, beyond Newfoundland, across the ocean towards Bermuda, the West Indies, and the old country if we have to. You're wondering who we are? We're just as good as the men of Saint Malo; we're people who can sail for Europe and plant the cross there. And with Your Excellency's blessing nothing can stop us now. We will be free men who sail the seven seas."

The launching certainly marked an epoch in the history of the Trois-Rivières diocese and even in the history of the region as a whole. It took place in 1867, three and a half years before the death of Father Tourigny's assistant, poor Father Armour Lupien, who loved belles-lettres as well as the arts in general and who had been appointed parish-priest of Saint-Thuribe pending his nomination to a Laval University

15

professorship which he never got. By then, however, *The Saint Elias* had already crossed the Straits of Newfoundland.

CHAPTER 2

One must go back to the occupation of our country by the Germans during the winter of 1776-1777 in order to understand just who Dr. Fauteux was — a man held in high esteem both by Father Tourigny and everyone else in Batiscan, although he never attended mass and remained the steadfast political adversary of Bishop Laflèche. These Germans were mercenaries whose services were paid for by the British government to the Duke of Brunswick and the Prince of Hesse-Kassel at the rate of seven pounds a man. Their arrival antagonized the Bostonians who brought the point home at Saratoga in the spring of 1777. Still, the Germans remained unbiased and the regiment of Major-General von Riedesel went into winter quarters in the Trois-Rivières tract from Maskinongé to Sainte-Anne-de-la-Pérade, leaving no unpleasant memories there. After Saratoga, when the troops were to be repatriated, they had dispersed all over the countryside, settling down in the United States or in Canada where several of them were assimilated into the French community. The subsequent adventures of Major-General von Riedesel give one a fair idea of their state of mind.

The Major-General had left his wife in Europe in

an interesting condition. Shortly after her delivery she crossed the Atlantic and arrived in Trois-Rivières in the spring of 1777. Not content with being accompanied by her three children Gustavus, Frederica and Caroline, she would not rest until she had joined her husband. She was a young, good-humoured, even-tempered woman and in spite of war, defeat and the fact that her husband's regiment had been wiped out, she was to find ways and means of adding two little girls to his progeny, the first of which was born in our country and baptized, "Canada," the second being born in the United States and christened "America." Although both these names were quite appropriate, they nevertheless bore witness to a certain indifference concerning the war which the Major-General had been prosecuting.

During a visit to the Ursuline hospital in Trois-Rivières, Lady von Riedesel was to notice the presence of a young man destined to become the ancestor of Doctor Fauteux. In one of the wards, a non-commissioned officer wearing the uniform of Prince Frederick threw himself at her feet. She was bewildered. Well dressed, reserved, he hadn't looked like a patient at all.

"Save me, madam!" he cried out.

She would have gladly done so, but how could she? She didn't even know his name and asked him what it was. Still kneeling at her feet he answered that he was called Faustus.

"Faustus?"

"Yes, madam."

Adding with his hands clasped: "Murder me, for mercy's sake, madam, so that I may return to Germany."

The request was strange enough, especially coming

18

from a young non-com whose name reminded her of her childhood, Salzburg puppet shows, the very heart of her country.

"I will not forget you, Faustus," said Lady von Riedesel.

She stood before him as if she had something more to say, moving her lips and finding nothing to add. Finally, deeply moved, she took some money from her purse, handed it to him and suddenly walked away while the handsome officer bowed low before the woman who was no longer there when he looked up. Then, before the nuns who were all atwitter, the distinguished young man flung the coins into the air, laughing hysterically.

"Take me out of here. Take me out of here quickly," said Lady von Riedesel whom the Ursulines spirited away to a small room adjoining the ward from which she still heard the laughter of the young officer who wore the uniform of Prince Frederick. She was unable to recover there.

"Take me out," she repeated, almost beside herself.

The man she had promised never to forget kept haunting her. Each time she remembered him, she was afraid of feeling faint. But how could she help him? Her husband, the Major-General had enough cares and worries as it was and she didn't dare burden him with hers. She spoke about it to the dean, Father Saint-Onge.

"But you are not going to exorcize him, are you? You won't find a fiend of hell in him and have him burned at the stake?"

"Why should we? He is a young gentleman and we have more than enough girls in our parishes."

Lady von Riedesel laughed so much that tears were

streaming down her cheeks.

"Why are you laughing, madam?" the dean asked her.

"How was I to know..."

She couldn't stop giggling.

"... to know you were human? I've heard so many tales about the papists."

"Don't you think that I haven't heard as many about the heretics, my Lady?" answered the dean.

He did not laugh. He was glum. Lady von Riedesel, with characteristic warmth held the prelate's hand and said to him:

"Don't be so depressed. You can cure him if you want to."

"My Lady, who do you think I am? Do you not know that these words were once said to our Lord?"

"Well, do I or do you represent him here?"

The dean bowed deeply before her and when he stood erect again, Lady von Riedesel had already moved away. She had made her point and he could hear her laughter. She was running, she was happy and the dean was no longer depressed. He even smiled as nothing seemed easier to him than to bring Faustus to his right senses.

"I will fast if need be."

He received the young non-com who hurled himself at his feet, as he had done before the General's wife.

"For mercy's sake, Sir, kill me so that I may return to Germany."

Lady von Riedesel had been moved but the dean stood like a rock.

"We've had enough of this nonsense," he said and the NCO picked himself up, confused, apprehensive, grinning like a child who has been found out and doesn't really mind the fact that adults aren't total idiots, since as a potential adult he would eventually become the victim of today's lies and deceits. Show him up for what he is, deliver him from his own nature and his grin is a contented one. The dean ordered the young man to be stripped of his uniform.

"You have no right," he protested.

"Now you're talking. But you are quite mistaken, my boy. How can you claim any right to this German uniform when you are involved in a war between the British and the Americans?"

"No matter. Do not take it from me. I beg of you."

The dean answered:

"Master Faustus, you should make the best of a bad job. There is no Prince Frederick here and this is not Germany. You are in Canada, sir, and you will dress like a *Canadien*."

He had him dressed according to local fashion. The poor young gentleman lost much of the charming distinction which had caught the eye of Lady von Riedesel and the dean then sent him to improve his French in a settler's household on the outskirts of Machiche.

"Godspeed, master Faustus and may we not hear from you before two or three generations."

"But the general's wife, Your Excellency?"

"I have lent her my carriage so that she may join and comfort her husband before the battle which will take place in the vicinity of Lake Champlain."

On the outskirts of Machiche the young non-commissioned officer learned the language well enough to marry one of the settler's daughters in the course of the next year. He had signed François Fausteus in the parish register but his name was altered further still. As far back as 1789, in the account books

21

of M. Duplessis, miller of Pointe-du-Lac, he had become François Fauteux. As such the name has endured from one generation to the next, until now. Having brought up ten children, his wife who was called Marie-Josephte Caron, died. She'd had a considerable hold on him and he lived on, after a fashion, for five years. He had a peculiar habit of standing near the intersection of the road and his sloping pathway which led up to it, waiting, as he said, for the dean's carriage. The ecclesiastic had died long before and people let him be since the whole thing was considered unimportant. They shrugged and said:

"Well, he's German."

His children scattered all about the country, one of them, who could only speak French, travelling down to New York where he worked as a typographer in a print shop which put out nothing but French and Dutch publications. This man's only son studied medicine in New York and returned to settle down in Batiscan some years before Father Elias Tourigny held forth there. In 1869, he had been practising for so long that in the eyes of many he seemed to have been the local doctor since time immemorial. His name, like that of his ancestor, was François. He had brought from the United States both his diploma and a self-reliance which could have made things uncomfortable for him at the beginning of his career had it not been for his rank as well as the good services he rendered. He never did attend mass, but what's worse, had belonged to the *Patriote* party and this didn't go down well at all in the Trois-Rivières diocese. Age didn't bring him to alter his commitments. However, no one could hurt him then.

"He's a member of the *Institut Canadien*. When Papineau, Dessaules, Dourtre or Dorion come here, he provides them with food and lodging in his home.''

''Listen to me, Armour Lupien...''

''He introduces them when they speak on the church steps.''

''Don't you think I know?''

''They hold these meetings after mass, flouting the authority of the Church. He must be dealt with!''

''Dr. Fauteux has lived here longer than I have, young man, and he isn't just a practitioner barely competent to sign death certificates. He knows how to treat his patients and he knows how to cure them. What's more he is the most renowned obstetrician from Trois-Rivières to Grondines. Never even say a word against him. The Lord has not sent you here so that you may stir up a scandal in my parish. And remember this, one must never demand from a man more than he can do.''

Father Armour Lupien looked down, not knowing what to say for a moment. Suddenly, the young assistant stared defiantly into the priest's face.

''Does His Excellency Bishop Laflèche agree?''

Father Elias Tourigny answered slowly like a man whose words carry weight and are carefully thought out.

''What His Excellency thinks is irrelevant. Furthermore, there is one master here, sir, and it is not Bishop Laflèche, it is me.''

Father Lupien considered himself forewarned and never mentioned the doctor again although he hated the very sight of the man. He tried to incriminate him indirectly by indicting Philippe Cossette, a prosperous farmer and owner of the toll-bridge which spanned the Batiscan River. As will be seen later on God did punish him for that. It even proved to be the true

23

cause of his death when he had become the pastor of Saint-Thuribe, pending his nomination as professor of letters at Laval University which had been agreed to by Bishop Caron and Father Tourigny, precisely on the evening of the afore-mentioned launching. Both men, brokers of the soul so to speak, had agreed that the young priest's *forte* was not a parish ministry. He was a poet, a philosopher and had to be provided with a professorship as soon as possible.

"You may keep him for a year or two," Bishop Caron had said. "I then will find him a small parish according to the custom of the diocese."

"The custom?" asked the Canon.

"You didn't know? The custom according to which Father Tourigny's assistants are invariably appointed to a parish when leaving Batiscan. He won't be the man for it but it will silence the envious when he'll be transferred to Laval later on... In which faculty, Theology? Letters?"

"Letters, Your Excellency, Letters."

"Are you quite sure?"

"I'm afraid he is too much the little ecclesiastic to have it in him. He overdoes things."

"I have not considered his case in those terms," said Bishop Caron. "You may be right, however."

Thus the career of Father Armour Lupien was settled.

"He is not an emeritus professor as of now," observed the prelate.

"I'm afraid I disagree with your appointing him to a parish. He will achieve nothing or overdo it there and may simply end up moping."

"Then, mope he will, God willing."

Bishop Charles-Olivier Caron had finished cleaning his pipe and was now about to go to bed. Father

Tourigny did not share his submissiveness to the divine will.

"He is a priest who brings an endowment with him, I know that."

"Yes, because of his mother."

"I know that too. I wonder exactly why you required an endowment. He will either peter out young or live on to a ripe old age. I don't like this business of a little parish by which he must earn his appointment to the university. Precisely because of his mother's illness. Extravagance is one of the side-effects, you know."

"I thought I had noticed... Father, one can't foresee everything when managing a diocese unless one wants to go crazy. You define guidelines to the best of your knowledge and then apply them. Your assistant will have his parish come what may. Are you aware that plenty of fresh air often does wonders in these cases?"

His Excellency Charles-Olivier took one of the candlesticks which were at the foot of the stairs, lit the candle and went upstairs.

CHAPTER 3

When Bishop Laflèche died, his praises were not sung unanimously. On the contrary, his career was reassessed and even his missionary work wasn't highly regarded. It was compared with that of Father Lacombe who had been poor among the poor, as ingenuous as a child, who had sensed the meekness of the people and never preached to them the existence of hell other than the slaughtering of the last buffalo. Laflèche had apparently been quite the opposite, handling the crucifix like a sword, passionately fond of gloomy visions and as overbearing as a Spaniard. Of all the letters which he wrote out West, the best deals with the description of a battle. As Bishop of Trois-Rivières he still behaved like an autocrat, though he was careful to do so only when dealing in generalities and avoided offending his constituents who would otherwise have jumped down his throat. His foolish and notorious extravagance therefore showed itself exclusively outside of his diocese.

His enemies even went so far as to slander his successor-to-be:

"Should Canon Cloutier inherit his pastoral staff it would justify the opinion of those who claim that Trois-Rivières was an afterthought, created on the eighth day... The Maskinongé schism would proliferate and we would find ourselves with a second, if diminutive Laflèche which would prove very prejudicial to the memory of the deceased.''

In fact, Bishop Cloutier was a mediocre prelate who, towards the end of his life had to be provided with a coadjutor. He retired to the Sisters of Providence hospice. My father was his altar boy. Each morning the man would hide, either in a wall cupboard or under his bed and had to be dragged out and brought to the holy altar. No one remembers him now except members of his own family who are indebted to him — even the Hon. François Cloutier — since His Excellency's only talents were for nepotism.

The Church then had enormous political power, but did not know how to apply it since such power was really superfluous to its role. This mad, incoherent power consisting in contradictory policies whose single aim was to demonstrate its existence had only been used in the abstract by Bishop Laflèche, his true successors being Bishop Bernard of Saint-Hyacinthe and Archbishop Paul Bruchési of Montreal. Judge D. Monet used to tell a characteristic anecdote. There already was an excellent college in Iberville called Sainte-Marie du Monnoir. It was said that His Excellency wanted to close it down and build another. The judge went to see the archbishop who took him by the arm round the living room of the archiepiscopal palace.

''What do you think, sir. Are these the walls of an archbishop's palace? Would you say they were appropriate?''

There were a few small cracks in the plaster, not much to speak of, the proof being that today, sixty years later, the living room is still standing. Judge

Monet answered His Excellency that he didn't consider himself an authority on decorum. On the other hand, would His Excellency be kind enough to explain the drift of his remark?

"What I mean, Your Honor, is that I haven't a sou to spend on a college in Saint-Jean. I would rather have the episcopal palace walls rebuilt first so it may be worthy of the Archbishop of Montreal."

Six months later, His Excellency came riding hell for leather into Saint-Jean declaring:

"I'll provide you with a classical college even if you already have one and I am giving it to you because I must have my very own."

This insane, harmful dominion of a national Church oblivious to its true function and willingly manipulated by the diplomats of the Vatican hovered, perhaps, over the diocese of Trois-Rivières during Bishop Laflèche's tenure of office but never descended upon it as it did in Montreal during the reign of Archbishop Paul Bruchési and that of Cardinal Léger. His Excellency was noticed at a distance and aroused a certain hostility but in fact his authority was too remote to be real. He was never more than the weathercock of the diocese, spinning round above his cathedral, unable to keep the sextons and beadles from doing things their way or His Excellency Charles-Olivier Caron from being the master of the palace and managing the routine of the diocese sensibly, with the assent of the pastors who themselves complied with the decisions of the church overseers who managed their parishioners.

In Batiscan, Doctor Fauteux who foresaw the consequences of episcopal autocracy was the professed adversary of Bishop Laflèche. His Excellency was offended but couldn't retaliate except by having the

Sisters of the Precious Blood pray for his conversion. But when all was said and done, he respected the old doctor. No one in Batiscan ever would have uttered a word against him whether from the pulpit or in the depths of the vestry. Father Tourigny cautioned all of his new assistants.

"You have just graduated from the seminary. It goes without saying that you are under the dominant influence of your bishop but you are now in my presbytery and I am the boss here. You have learned to seek the kingdom of God in the abstract, you are now going to bring it about in actual fact. I don't want to hear about the Zouaves. Their baggy pants are ludicrous. And please give those who don't agree with His Excellency the right to freedom of speech."

His unsophisticated assistants would stare at him, astonished. How could one not agree with His Excellency?

"What he says is beyond the majority of my parishioners and as irrelevant to them as the clouds above. But, some consider him an autocrat, Doctor Fauteux in particular. Well, I'm warning you, don't even breathe a word against him: first, because the parish couldn't do without him; second, because his good services and his dedication should be acknowledged."

Canon Elias Tourigny who had no inclination at all for contentiousness valued the doctor as a man and considered him a friend. Had he had to choose between him and Bishop Laflèche he would have discarded His Excellency. He didn't say so to his assistants since he considered them good, lumpish oafs who were not to be unduly disturbed. Moreover, he was not without misgivings himself as he wanted to abide by his Bishop although he was unwilling to compromise his rights as a lifetime pastor. He dreaded the excesses of both men and did not for the world wish to find himself in a position where he would have to choose between them. The priest and the doctor had often met at the bedside of the sick, hardly able to exchange more than civil greetings. Yet, so it was that they acquired the habit of forbearance which was to evolve into a friendly relationship.

One day they met as if by accident on the wooden footpath of the village when both were out for a walk. It was during hay-making and since everyone in the parish was too busy to call on either, both were on holiday. For the first time in many years, after more than a quarter of a century, they spoke man to man, saying more or less this — the conversation taking place before the arrival of Father Armour Lupien and the launching of the three-master which took place almost simultaneously.

"Canon Tourigny," said Doctor Fauteux, "we always have gotten along fairly well although we've never been particularly close. We may not have had much to say to each other but I'm afraid time is running short and we should now come to an agreement if you care to."

"I am certainly willing, doctor, but since I am not a member of a one-man church there are rules and regulations which I must comply with. An agreement. At this point, an agreement would only concern your soul, I take it? I wouldn't claim not to be interested. May I only point out that since the death of your wife your pew, near the main aisle, has remained vacant."

"My wife is still occupying it. Don't you see her? I always respected her piety. Why should I stop doing so now that she is dead?"

"You could accompany her occasionally."

"You know that my work doesn't allow…"

"That's the explanation we usually give, that you don't have enough time to spare to attend mass. No one is offended. What's worse, however, is that each year Low Sunday goes by and one of our parishioners hasn't done his Easter duty."

"How could that possibly be? I never heard the knell."

"You have no hand in it doctor, I have taken the fault upon myself. You don't only treat your patients well, you also show concern for their faith."

"How strange of you to mention it. Why should I deprive them of a belief which helps them live?"

The pastor stood there, abstracted, taking a few steps without saying a word.

"What about our agreement?"

"What kind of an agreement, doctor? I must say that I am somewhat on my guard."

"Do you think that I mistake you for the devil?"

"You'd be the man to do it! No. You see, I'm on my guard because I have to handle you with kid gloves. Do you know how I answer those who worry over your soul because your political creed isn't exactly that of Bishop Laflèche? I ask them who in this parish has best put into practice God's greatest commandment."

"Yes, I have been told… But didn't you once claim that I was of German descent and that German attitudes might be different from *ours*?"

"I did. But that was a long time ago. Besides I was hedging; I simply never felt qualified to pass judgment on you. I was trying not to upset my parishioners. I have always tried to keep them from choosing between either one of us.

"As to our agreement: I want to be buried in conse-

crated ground beside my wife. What would be required of me for a fine funeral?''

''To prepare yourself for death.''

''That depends. I wouldn't advise you to rush in
with the sprinkler as soon as the first symptoms of
illness manifest themselves.''

''Don't worry, doctor, we will be very discreet.
Call on me when you are unconscious, on the brink of
death, and I'll come running. All the same, don't wait
until you're past praying for.''

''We will do what we can, Father.''

''Then, it's settled, isn't it.''

''Thank you, my friend.'' said Doctor Fauteux.

This momentous agreement was ratified in the
Trois-Rivières bishop's palace by His Excellency
Charles-Olivier Caron, a man of God, easier to deal
with than Bishop Laflèche who was a born politician
and thus had earned himself a considerable reputation
as well as the curtailment of his diocese. Bishop
Caron attended to more serious matters, particularly
the training of candidates for the priesthood. He had
noticed that the seminary wouldn't do and considered
a period of probation in certain parishes, particularly
in Batiscan, essential. Canon Elias Tourigny was very
good at rounding off the edges of theology, edges
which cut the faithful to the quick, making them flare
up against the holiest authorities and sometimes dis-
sent, as had been the case in Baie-du-Fève and
Maskinongé. Because of this knack, every second
year he was assigned one, sometimes two and even
three assistants who were certain of being appointed
as pastors of a parish later on.

After the launching of the three-master — destined
to throw open the gate which had excluded our people
from world history — His Excellency Charles-Olivier

had gone up to bed no longer thinking about this ship which was the emblem of freedom. Nor did it engross the mind of Father Elias Tourigny in whose honor it had been christened *The Saint Elias*. However, instead of retiring, he had stayed awake, preoccupied by his new assistant, Father Armour Lupien. He wasn't all that sure that the young priest's stay in Batiscan was going to help him learn the score and finish the education he had received at the Trois-Rivières seminary. He was one of those rare persons to whom solid reality meant little — something that was never to be deferred to — but who on the other hand, never stop bending facts to their will as long as they live, thanks to the nature and power of their ideas. If they survive, they grow into artists, saints, psychopaths or criminals. Driven by a frightening ambition they become powerful and deadly thanks to their capacity for achieving affluence and social status. The young man tended to behave this way because of a particular endowment of course, but thanks to his educational background as well. Since he had been weaned early and hadn't had a mother's love, he was desperately unsociable. Father Tourigny wondered how he could get across to him and bless him with ''the peace which passeth all understanding.'' Father Lupien had promised him not to mention Dr. Fauteux when speaking from the pulpit. The canon never doubted that he would keep his word and was equally certain that he would find some way of striking at him indirectly.

''Jesus! why, why did they send me that creature? I don't know a thing about wild animals. Why didn't they put me in charge of a calf well-fed from birth, who's had all the tender loving care he can take?''

Florence, his housekeeper, showed her face in the kitchen. She wanted the pastor to know that since she had gotten out of bed before him and she would also go to sleep after he had, as usual, she just didn't want to spend the night standing there.

"Florence. I'd forgotten you. Very well, up we go... I'm worried about the new assistant. Do you think I can make a pastor out of him who will bring peace and harmony to his parish?"

"Why ask me? He hasn't even looked at me since he's been here."

She faltered a little before advising Canon Tourigny to ask Philippe Cossette, the owner of the toll-bridge instead.

"He's often over at his place."

"Yes, so I have been told."

"... even when Philippe Cossette isn't in."

The canon took his candlestick and lit the candle. At the foot of the stairs he listened to the snores of Bishop Charles-Olivier who had fallen asleep as soon as he had retired.

"That's His Excellency. What do you think of him, Florence?"

"His Excellency is a servant of the Lord. He sleeps by night and prays by day and doesn't worry over a wolf prowling around the sheepfold."

"But what about the sheep, Florence, the defenseless sheep?"

"The defenseless sheep, my eye. If I were you I'd worry more about the wolf."

Canon Tourigny went up, candlestick in hand. It was obvious that Florence didn't think much of Marguerite, Philippe Cossette's wife, which wasn't unexpected since Florence considered slandering all the women in the parish her strong point. Marguerite was somewhat more conspicuous than most. She had fiery slit-like eyes, full, black, opulent hair and was still childless after three years of married life. Although he was fat, Philippe Cossette the owner of the toll-bridge and the most prosperous farmer from Champlain to La Pérade was then perhaps not that chaste. His fine wife wasn't one of the girls offered him in marriage after his mother's death. He had gone to fetch her up-stream of the Rivière des Envies beyond the lands of the local vintage families, in an area where lines of descent are totally confused and you find people who migrated from the western part of the province and crossed the Saint-Maurice in Sainte-Flore. Here the neglected and questionable offspring of the Marchands and the Massicottes are called Pagnol and here halfbreeds from the north may have slipped in. The uncertain origin of the population added to Marguerite's attractiveness. When Philippe Cossette came to the presbytery for the publishing of the banns, the priest asked him if he knew just what kind of girl he was marrying.

"Yes." Philippe Cossette had answered.

"Then, my boy, let me tell you that you are absolutely right to do it."

However he'd never had any children, although Marguerite had made him get to work and turned him into a competitive businessman. He had become so powerful, could throw so much weight around, was the expression used, that no one in the older parishes would have dared to insinuate that she was a halfbreed. Doctor Fauteux who hadn't quite known what to do with his free time since his wife's death was always dropping in at his house. If he hadn't been so old there would have been rumors of his having an affair.

The news which Canon Tourigny had just learned from his housekeeper didn't help him drop off to sleep. He felt apprehensive over the meeting of Dr. Fauteux and Father Lupien at Philippe Cossette's and wished he were snoring away like His Excellency.

"Lord, make my spirit yours," he said, "and grant that I may come to love men and the earth as he does, sufficiently, so to achieve detachment and go to sleep when I want to."

CHAPTER 4

The Saint Elias had already sailed the high seas several times beyond the Straits of Newfoundland and Pierre Maheu, its captain, who wasn't a native of the village was becoming very popular there, especially among the young. He had been chosen to bring to a successful issue the expeditions of this great sailing ship which was the pride of the parish, and been considered more suitable than local seafaring men like C.D.A. Massicotte or J.D.C. Trudel (they were located on main street and could hire out wherever they pleased, even in Champlain), because he had done less coastwise trade and more knocking about than they had, particularly when working for British magnates whose ships ploughed the world's seas. People had at first thought that *The Saint Elias* belonged to a corporation of notables. It was later realized that, coincidentally, its sole owner had been Maheu's lifelong friend; he was nicknamed Mithridates and was Philippe Cossette.

The nickname had been given him by Father Armour Lupien who had promised Father Tourigny never to utter from the pulpit the name of Dr. Fauteux, leader of the faction opposed to the policies of Bishop Laflèche. For Father Lupien who was then just out of the seminary, these policies were the Church's, indeed God's own. He was a rousing preacher whom the parish priest enjoyed listening to, although he didn't consider him reliable, doctrinally speaking, and wouldn't let him preach when ecclesiastics visited the parish, out of a fear of being denounced. Father Lupien did not only preach on the Papacy — his Holiness being on the horns of a dilemma in his States, Father Lupien nursed a grudge on his account against the reds and the Garibaldians — but on the Godhead as well, which he conceived of in terms not offensive to Canon Tourigny who nevertheless wouldn't have vouched for their soundness.

"It is the Father" he would say, "who proceeded from the Son, and the Father created the canopy of heaven for us out of gratefulness."

When his assistant preached on this theme which he seemed to dote on, the canon from his bench in the chancel glanced at the nave, hoping to catch sight of Dr. Fauteux there in his reserved seat. However the bench always remained vacant and the canon, feeling aggravated, wondered whether he shouldn't excommunicate the doctor. He would have enjoyed so much discussing his assistant's sermon with him afterwards. Dr. Fauteux was the only man in the world with whom he could possibly do so, and he was never there.

"I shall excommunicate him," he would say out of resentment, quite conscious that he didn't intend to and that he had, on the contrary, promised to bury him in consecrated ground beside his pious wife.

"When Low Sunday comes round the knell will toll from morning till night."

On the other hand, he felt very glad that the pew

40

was vacant whenever Father Lupien tackled more down-to-earth issues and spoke like an inquisitor because his beloved father the Pope, adverse to the principle of nationalism, dead-set against progress and history, was in something of a predicament in Rome minus the Papal States. According to Father Lupien who even then demonstrated the inanity of the Church's political power, he should have headed a world empire and been more imperial than Caesar himself. It was during one of these wild extempore declarations that he described the sorrow of his Excellency, Bishop Laflèche, at having black sheep in his flock.

"The fool is going to name him!" thought Canon Tourigny.

He didn't mention Dr. Fauteux by name but declared that the infamous Garibaldi even had his henchmen in the fine parish of Batiscan.

"Go to the dwelling of Mithridates, King of Pontus, and you shall see them conspiring in secrecy..."

He then turned towards the celebrant who was afflicted with a seemingly endless coughing fit. The celebrant stopped coughing and spoke out.

"Father Lupien, please make a long story short. I have caught this grippe from you and would like to get the mass over with as soon as possible."

Even before Canon Tourigny's intervention, everyone present had understood the pointed allusion to Cossette, the owner of the toll-bridge at whose house Dr. Fauteux was a frequent caller. The name Mithridates had never been pronounced before in Batiscan since the beginning of the world. It seemed both peculiar and amusing and everyone tried to make up for lost time. It was repeated *ad nauseam* as everyone thought it suited Philippe Cossette who

41

was rather well off, particularly well off. From then on, everybody referred to him as "King Mithridates."

Two men came out of church furious after high mass, Father Tourigny and the new King of Pontus; the first more than the second, since Cossette headed for home plagued by uncertainty, anxious to find out what Dr. Fauteux' opinion was.

"Is the doctor here?"

"You know he isn't, Philippe," answered Marguerite. "Every Sunday he has to be available to those who come to mass."

"Why are you calling me Philippe? That pint-sized excuse for an assistant orating in the pulpit has just claimed my name's Mithridates."

Philippe Cossette's young wife let out a laugh.

"Made a fool out of me too."

"Philippe, you poor thing."

"My name ain't Philippe, it's King Mithridates."

"So, you're a king now? Well, that isn't so bad and between you and me it's rather true."

"You dont' know what you're talking about. If you even knew who this damned Mithridates was! But you don't. Nobody does in town except little smart-ass Armour Lupien, Father Tourigny, and the doctor who is always here when I don't need him and isn't when I do. Marguerite, next time you meet him tell the doctor I just don't want to see him around here any more."

"Tell him yourself, Philippe Cossette."

The toll-collector, the ship-owner, the well-to-do farmer let himself sink into his armchair.

"I don't feel good, Marguerite. Go and get the doctor."

"Poor sweet thing, you're much worse off than

you think. You don't need a doctor you need a priest. I'll send the maid to the presbytery.''

The king bounced back to his feet.

''I'll brain you if you do.''

''Any time, Philippe. Be my guest.''

Cossette had been his mother's good little boy for too long to tackle his beautiful, headstrong wife. He slumped back into his seat and Marguerite rang for the maid, who wasn't far off, as was to be expected.

''Aurilda, go to Dr. Fauteux's home and tell him monsieur Cossette doesn't feel well — in private so no one will overhear you. Above all he mustn't rush over since Father Lupien would just love it if he did. Tell him exactly what happened. Tell him this damned curate has nicknamed my husband Mithridates and we would like to know what the word means before we get good and mad.''

''Thanks Marguerite. You're more precious to me than a queen.''

She patted him on the head.

''Yes, my king. Yes, my Mithridates.''

Then, both went up to bed and lost count of time, somewhat. When she felt that she could go up without embarrassing them, Aurilda came to say that the doctor as well as Father Lupien were waiting in the livingroom.

''But, Aurilda we haven't had lunch yet.''

''Dinner is ready.''

''Well, now. Invite them both to eat with us.''

Philippe Cossette soon had nothing but his frock-coat to slip on.

''Marguerite, get dressed. What are you waiting for?''

''Dear, I've heard that in Paris women entertain

43

their guests wearing a nightgown, in deshabille, as they say."

"This is not Paris, this is Batiscan."

"Don't you know the doctor treated me when I was sick and I don't have a thing to hide from him?"

"Marguerite, the assistant..."

"Your majesty, you're too good to be true."

Philippe couldn't help laughing. Above all, he couldn't conceal the affection he felt for his young and pretty wife who loved him in turn and was only unfaithful to him on doctor's orders, so as to give him children and to love him even more.

It was later than two o'clock in the afternoon, yet no one had eaten: Philippe and Marguerite because they had been sleeping; the doctor because he had come as soon as he had hurried through his Sunday morning consultations; and Father Lupien, because in the presbytery he had found Canon Tourigny in a towering passion worse than that of Moses coming down from Sinai. The canon, his face flushed, had hollered at him:

"So you take me for a superannuated idiot, do you! You overrule my veto through malicious expedients which can lend themselves to every possible misinterpretation! 'Mithridates, king of Pontus.' Very smart. Of course everyone understood you were referring to Cossette, the owner of the bridge, and that your accusations were in fact aimed at Dr. Fauteux since Cossette hasn't got the shadow of a political idea in his head. You have both disobeyed me and nicknamed an individual who didn't deserve it, a man whose business sense has proved useful to this parish."

"Nicknamed?"

"You are abstruse, bookish, totally unable to make yourself understood by plain folks. No one in this village even suspects who Mithridates was. Now, wouldn't you think that the word could stick and become his nickname?"

Father Lupien hung his head sheepishly.

"You will go, right now, to Mr. Cossette's residence to offer him your apologies and explain that the expression is in no way pejorative, since Mithridates spent the better part of his life fighting the Romans who were the Englishmen of their own day and time."

Father Armour Lupien therefore called at the home of Philippe Cossette. He was introduced into the livingroom, shortly after which Dr. Fauteux came in, out of breath.

"You may not believe this, Father, but I've been called upon in my capacity as a philologist rather than as a medical man. It's the first time since the beginning of my career... thanks to you, by the way, my arrogant young friend."

"That may very well be so, doctor."

"The terms involved must be considered within their local context. I had always thought the kingdom of Pontus idiotic. Here, everything becomes crystal clear: Pontus can only refer to the bridge of Philippe Cossette, the owner of several other assets, particularly of the magnificent three-master which has been launched recently and does honor to this village. If you compare him with others, and not just common laborers but farmers as well, you might say that he is a king... Between ourselves, Father, Philippe is as conceited as most men and will be flattered."

"You could also add, doctor, that Mithridates spent the better part of his life fighting the Romans who were the Englishmen of their day."

"In short, my dear Father Lupien, you never intended to insult my friend at all."

The priest grinned, letting his teeth show.

"No," he answered, "I was trying to get you."

The doctor seemed delighted by this candor.

"I've always loved my enemies when you come down to it. I feel diminished when they're mean and when they crawl. But why do it in this roundabout way?"

"Because of Canon Tourigny. He isn't an idealist, he just wants peace and harmony in his parish. Well, then, you've been around long enough to save lives and many feel grateful to you for having done it. I can't denounce your ideas without implicating you as a public figure. The canon is probably right but I'm young and I let myself be carried away by what I was saying."

The priest looked thin, bony, apparently in uncertain health, at once exhausted and hyperactive. He wasn't at all agreeable or engaging although not totally unattractive. Under thick-set, black eyebrows his blue eyes had a peculiar charm: eyes that might fascinate a woman, although neither she nor anyone else would ever tie him down. The old doctor couldn't help pitying him for his need of an absolute which seemed incompatible with life as he knew it. Still, he couldn't help thinking that Father Tourigny had the aptitudes required to bless Philippe Cossette with a son.

"Young man, you haven't a thing to worry about," Dr. Fauteux said. "My friends are going to be very straightforward about welcoming you here. I even wonder if you'll always require Father Tourigny's express orders to come here again."

"What do you mean?"

The assistant felt ill at ease. The old doctor's words which were fraught with mental reservations had left him peculiarly ill at ease. Shortly after, Philippe and Marguerite came down and everybody went to the dining room, Father Lupien apoligizing hastily and Dr. Fauteux adding a few words on the subject. A sweet, pale, mulled wine was served. During the meal the eyes of the young ecclesiastic and the young woman, which were strikingly unlike, met and both were confused, astonished even, by the passion they felt for each other. Philippe Cossette thought it was aversion. Dr. Fauteux saw things as they were and perhaps as he had wanted them to be but still felt miserable because he was on friendly terms with the canon. As to Mithridates, King of Pontus, nothing more was said about him except to lament his downfall, his poisons and his death.

"We'll try to go one better," said Philippe Cossette raising his glass, which showed that there were no hard feelings between him and Father Lupien and that the assistant when innocently enough crowning Mithridates the First from the pulpit had given birth to a dynasty in whose second generation his lineage and Marguerite's would manifest itself.

CHAPTER 5

Mithridates II was christened Armour Cossette in his parents' residence, near the toll-bridge which on that day had its gate up, open to all comers by way of public rejoicing. The baptism took place at home on pretext that the child's frail health didn't allow him to become a Christian as all the children of Batiscan had before him and would do after, at the baptismal font of the parish church.

Canon Tourigny didn't attend this ceremony, the officiant being a priest from the Trois-Rivières diocese, Father Normand, then considered successor-apparent to Bishop Laflèche as he was later to be that of Bishop Cloutier. The Father never had any title to boast of other than such rumors: not only did he never become a bishop but he didn't even earn himself a canon's cincture. Moreover, everyone in the village knew that the child was as sturdy as a newborn could possibly be and that his voraciousness delighted his father when little Armour compelled Marguerite to undo her shirt so as to nurse him. Dr. Fauteux, in spite of his age had insisted on being his godfather.

The Saint Elias had returned from a long voyage some time before this baptism. Coming ashore, Captain Maheu had said that he was proud of himself, his ship and the crew, because he'd done what had never been done before, making his way around the "triangle" counterclockwise. It was certainly an exploit and Captain Maheu was congratulated although just what the achievement consisted in wasn't that clear.

"The Saint Elias arrived" said Florence to the parish-priest, "and wouldn't you know, it went round the triangle counterclockwise."

The canon who had accompanied his curate to Saint-Thuribe where he'd been appointed pastor did not comment on the news. Everyone soon found out what the itinerary of the ship had been. It had brought back nothing but wines and spirits in its cargo holds — plenty of both, as much as it could carry — which meant that it was returning from the old country. One Batiscanese crew-member confirmed it.

"You won't believe this but they speak just about like we do over there, in French."

Part of the cargo went to the Church and part to the politicians. There were even some bottles of champagne. Champagne was served on the occasion of the baptism and Father Normand found the flavor just delightful. On his way back to Trois-Rivières he was lounging in the bishop's carriage as nonchalantly as a triumphant Roman conqueror and refused no one his blessing, not even the cows and pigs, "the poor forsaken ones" he said to the reticent coachman who sat ramrod-straight so as to make amends and restore the honor of His Excellency's coat of arms. In his heart of hearts, this ceremonious man had instinctively understood then that in spite of his noble bearing and his relatives, Father Normand would never become the Bishop of Trois-Rivières.

Beyond the Straits of Newfoundland, *The Saint*

Elias had sailed down to the West Indies, more exactly Cape Haiti, from which it had headed for La Rochelle harbor and then made its way back to Batiscan. In the past, French ships would sail down to Africa for a load of ebony, cross the Atlantic and then return to their home port. This was the triangle Captain Maheu had been referring to when he said that he had sailed it counterclockwise. His voyage certainly had been profitable for the ship's owner, Philippe Cossette alias Mithridates I. The baptism of his son, the second in the dynasty, had been celebrated at home which just wasn't done in Batiscan or the other parishes of the diocese. The waiving of the rules may have originated in a large shipment of mass wine sold at a rock-bottom price.

Four years later, the pastor of Saint-Thuribe had only six months of parish work left to do before becoming a professor of Letters at Laval University in Quebec City. He had found it rough going, since in spite of his eloquence and the artlessness he tried to achieve, he didn't talk like his parishioners. They tried to understand what he was saying and sweated it out but couldn't do it. He could see them strain and couldn't forgive himself. He felt absolutely wretched over his parish work although he consoled himself that in the faculty of Letters at least he would be understood. The thought was cold comfort to him since God did not become incarnate for bachelors of arts but for children and the simple-minded. He was considered a distinguished intellect; however he despised himself and but for divine grace would have regretted that he hadn't committed suicide by hanging and gotten it over with, in the barn of the Batiscan church vestry. However, he had already begun preparing his lectures which showed that his future career appealed to him. There, at least, he would make himself understood. His mentors, Charles-Olivier Caron and Canon Tourigny, may have known better what was good for him than he did himself. He was now reading Rotrou whose work he loved, even more than the great Corneille's.

Never pine for the world illusory delight
For t'is a baneful scourge to the children of light
Seemingly unswerving, forever inconstant
It both is and is not in a single instant

It was precisely because he thought himself unworthy of being God's representative on earth that he was drawn to both these men who possessed authority and who were old enough to be his father. He was grateful to them for having singled him out for distinction from among many others, for wishing him well and understanding him perhaps better than he understood himself. Above all he liked the canon, not so much because he'd saved his life at a time when he would rather have died, but for giving him a second chance and for providing him with a justification for his existence, if not the will to live.

Regrettably, he went no farther than Rotrou and never taught literature at Laval either. In the spring of 1873, he was suddenly carried off by a chest ailment he must have been nurturing for some time and which declared itself after he had caught a chill when going to perform the last rites for a poor old devil who lived on a side-road in Saint-Alban, replacing the local pastor who was away. He may have rushed òver too hastily. The man who was presumably dying was a sly old Magoua[1] who'd felt ill after a family quarrel.

---

[1] Magoua: member of an agricultural sub-proletariat.

When Armour Lupien arrived, exhausted, the man already felt better and was clamoring for his pipe.

"Hurry it up, Father, I've got to have a smoke."

Father Lupien wondered whether he hadn't taken a lot of trouble for nothing. Another man would have been indignant. He only felt stricken and didn't dare to think of the return trip. It was raining that night and the roads which had been frozen over were full of pot-holes. The sexton who was his coachman had advised him on arrival to hold on to the good Lord.

"No matter what, Linette is going to walk lame for a month and her legs'll be full of cuts and bruises."

This mare, a fine thoroughbred, had been Canon Tourigny's gift to his ex-assistant when he'd become the pastor of Saint-Thuribe.

"Hold on tight so she won't lacerate herself with her calks. I know a guy who'd be furious over this and so do you, Canon Tourigny. He judges a man by his horse and if he ever found Linette with her legs shot up he'd break both of yours, Father, believe you me."

Fortunately an old woman stood at the patient's bedside. When she sensed the despair of the young ecclesiastic who was already weary beyond recall and soaking wet she cut in forcefully to cheer him up.

"Don't let the looks of things fool you, Father, they're all the same. Not one of them who doesn't ask for his pipe before he keels over."

The old girl had nothing but a stump of a tooth in her mouth. It was as black as soot but still held and she seemed so sure of what she was saying that she would have cajoled the devil himself. Father Lupien was only too willing to believe her. He administered extreme unction to the man. There was a neighbor — not a day-laborer, a ditch-digger, a poor wretch or a

53

Magoua — but a real farmer, proud and prim like those of the old parishes. Moreover he was a church-warden as well as the owner of a large house and he offered to take the pastor in as a guest, an offer which the sexton advised him to accept.

"Come over and rest for an hour at least while we dry your clothes. They're soaking wet."

"Thank you," answered Father Lupien," but we have to be on our way now if we want to arrive in time for the Angelus and the mass. It's no use drying my clothes when it's still raining. They'll just get soaked all over again and we'll get even more of a chill."

The farmer insisted, saying that he shouldn't over-work his horse.

"Yours has small hooves. It's going to sink in every step of the way and hurt its legs."

"The good Lord and his holy Mother will watch over us on our way back. I came here under an obliga-tion which doesn't have priority over my duties as a pastor."

The churchwarden lowered his head. He had cer-tainly found the words of the young priest impressive but above all he felt disgraced over the allegedly dying man who'd hopped out of bed as soon as he had received extreme unction and was swinging away in his rocking chair now, smoking his pipe.

"You've saved me life," he told the priest. "That sacrament sure does wonders for a man. I feel much better'n I did. Everybody will know it too. Five, ten years from now I'll still be telling'em how you came over on the most godawful spring night, in spite of the rain and the roads all broken up and did a miracle for a poor man like me."

The priest didn't answer since he hadn't meant

to perform miracles when administering the last rites to him. He thought that he could have possibly done without the prayer for the dead. The canon had warned him of the paradoxical reactions which he might trigger off from time to time, adding:

"In Trois-Rivières, the Romans may or may not have told you this, but God's representative isn't God, you know. He does his duty according to the rites of the Church and shouldn't be surprised if the Lord sometimes overrules him. You should never, never contradict unusual phenomena which you may have brought about against your will. One can only be worthy of God by respecting him as manifested through men who are poor and often confused."

So the pastor of Saint-Thuribe went back through an icy downpour, in the middle of the night, down roads where Linette, his mare, jerked at the bit wanting to break into a trot. But the sexton, his hands numbed and possibly frozen, had to slacken her pace to keep her from tripping when the roadway which lay higher than the snow covering the fields broke up under her slender hooves. When the sexton couldn't stand the pain in his hands or his aching coccyx any longer he slackened his hold on the reins, tightening them again before Linette could stumble, thinking of Canon Tourigny who loved God as much as he did horses and whose dominion extended to the parishes of Saint-Thuribe and Saint-Alban. From the pulpit he had formulated a number of precepts which were then quoted as if they had been gospel truth; namely, that the Last Judgment would take place in the presence of all the animals of the earth which the Lord would listen to as attentively as he did to men and that several hypocrites would then be universally shown up for what they were.

"God isn't a circuit court judge. As you have found out they rule in favor of the man who can out-talk you. The Last Judgment won't be the same. The animals, the children, the half-wits are going to be there. No matter how eloquently hypocrites and pharisees may distort the truth their words will go in one ear of the Sovereign Judge and out the other because he will see the misery of wretched brutes, the twitching and anxious faces of children and half-wits who were objects of derision and mockery. You have to slaughter livestock to live but let me tell you that those who take an evil pleasure in the squeals of the pigs which echo all over the parish when they are killed during Advent will be condemned and will howl in hell themselves for all eternity."

Linette came off with a few scratches, which after such a ride at that time of the year was far from discreditable. The sexton who was exhausted but pleased with himself tended his mare's legs and rang the morning Angelus at the appointed time, at six o'clock. The farmers of Saint-Thuribe who had already begun doing their morning chores in the cattle-sheds meditated as usual. However, in the presbytery, Father Lupien chilled to the bone and shivering was putting on some warm clothes so as to keep up appearances. During mass, after the Credo, he nearly fainted. Having knelt with his head very low he felt the faintness leave him. He rose, turned towards the congregation which was small because it was a week-day and the filthy weather had kept many of the older ladies at home, and he asked it to pray God as well as the day's saint to help him finish his mass. In fact, he was able to see it through although he didn't administer holy communion to the faithful. Once in the presbytery he drank some hot broth and went up to bed stopping halfway up the stairs to tell his housekeeper not to worry.

"I'm just worn out," he said.

She wasn't so sure since his face was covered with beads of sweat and he was shivering. During the afternoon she went to eavesdrop several times at the door of his room. Now and again he was affected with a slight, sharp cough and he sometimes moaned. She could even hear him say.

"Jesus, help me, Jesus."

Was he dreaming? Calling for help because he couldn't breathe properly and seemed to suffocate? The housekeeper was wrong, however. In spite of the sleepless night he had just spent her pastor wasn't asleep. Had she been certain that this was so, she would have known that he was critically ill, that he might even have caught his death of cold by travelling to Saint-Alban unneccessarily for the sake of an old Magoua who wasn't worth it and didn't require the services of a priest any more than he did those of an Indian witch doctor. Apprehensive, resentful towards the old man, the old wretch, she thought that if there had been a medicine man around he would have been called on, not the parish priest of Saint-Thuribe.

"Maybe not. He'd have had to pay him. He got the priest free. Poor creature of the good God, poor martyr that he is."

She was inverting the elements of the parable: her parish priest had become the ewe searching out the good shepherd who was lost. In spite of her misgivings, the housekeeper waited until noon to open the door of the room. She had knocked and been acknowledged only by a murmur. When she stepped in, she realized that her anxiety hadn't been groundless.

"What are you waiting for, Father, dinner is served."

"My poor Isola, please forgive me but I think I should rest some more. I'll come down for supper."

The pastor's answer was punctuated by fits of coughing and the chattering of his teeth.

"You're awfully sick, aren't you."

"A bit of a fever perhaps, that's all there is to it."

"I'll get you some hot broth."

"No! Can't you see I'm in a sweat! Let me sleep. That's all I ask."

"You poor man, do you think I can't tell you're not even able to sleep?"

Then, with a start and speaking with the headtone which was so impressive from the pulpit even if what was said was being misunderstood:

"Get out Isola!" he said. "I want to be alone. Alone! Do you understand!"

The housekeeper left the room feeling compassion for this young priest who could have been her son who, although he was in a bad way, wanted neither care nor comfort, like an orphan who had been deprived of both and didn't know how to accept attention. She lost no time in calling for help and that very evening, thanks to the recurring cold weather which had hardened the roads, the doctor of Sainte-Anne-de-la-Pérade was in the presbytery. His diagnosis was pneumonia of the right lung and he declared that it was a hazardous life-and-death struggle.

"In a week you'll know which of the two has won out."

He prescribed the usual treatment and returned to Sainte-Anne where other cases awaited him. When thanked for his diligence and skill, he shrugged.

"I'm just doing my job," he said. "If in a case like this my diagnosis and my prognosis are exact it restores my self-confidence, puts new life into me because these cases are rarer than you think. Most of the time all we can do is reassure a patient while feeling uneasy over his uncertain complaint."

The doctor was rated highly by his colleagues, although he wasn't terribly well liked by the population, which found him blunt and not much of a healer; he was too frank when practising an art that requires rather less than more candor.

CHAPTER 6

In his room in the small, shabby presbytery of Saint-Thuribe, around the bed from which he was never to rise, women bent over Armour Lupien. There was Isola his housekeeper, a little maid-servant whose name he didn't know, Estelle and Marguerite. Behind all of these faces he was searching out another of which he had no recollection, his mother's. He had lost her when just turning three and she had faded from his memory, although her features must have been hidden behind all of the faces he saw which perhaps were only masks covering her own. His father had never remarried and had continued loving his young wife who was dead and yet still alive. Armour always had resented him for having lost her, as if he'd been responsible for her death. The priest may not have been altogether wrong as he had found himself separated from his young mother and left to the mercy of a tormented father who had never ceased to dwell on his misfortune.

The poor man who was sensitive and gentle could sense his son's feelings. He wasn't shocked as he still reproached himself for having lost his young wife who deserved to live more than he did. He was a harness-maker in Saint-Justin. The farmers who were particular considered him a skilful and hard-working craftsman so that the harness-maker wasn't even mentioned in the local variant of the folksong which describes how the devil coming out of hell to round up those he wants to deal with gets all of the village's notables and craftsmen into his carriage. Léon Gérin put it on record in his notes:

If in a parish one of the village's craftsmen is considered worthy of admiration and respect, his trade isn't mentioned in the devil's song, the devil being the avenger of the farmers who, it goes without saying, never climb into the carriage themselves.

Moreover, Armour Lupien's father ran the church choir with an authority which no one ever challenged because he wasn't conceited and did it in memory of his wife. Her maiden name had been Saint-Cyr. She came from a musical family and had played the church organ for some months after her marriage. Several of the older people from neighboring parishes sometimes attended mass in Saint-Justin. They came because of the choir and were often seen with eyes full of tears for no particular reason. When children asked their parents: "Why are the old strangers crying?" parents found it difficult to keep their feelings under control and their curt answer was that these people were idiots who had alienated themselves from their pastor and were probably bawling because they regretted having done so.

Bishop Gérin who was the pastor of Saint-Justin and the brother of Antoine Gérin-Lajoie, the well-known writer, had helped the harness-maker provide his son with an education in the Trois-Rivières seminary. After six years of classical studies Armour applied to go into holy orders. He was required to study philosphy for two more years to begin with. When he had done so he applied again. An endowment was then insisted on so that he wouldn't be dependent on the diocese if he became an invalid as might be expected considering the disease which had carried off his mother. This endowment was soon provided. Of course, Bishop Gérin as well as his brother contributed to it but so did several prominent citizens from the counties of Berthier and Maskinongé. Dr. Neveu of Sainte-Ursule, a bachelor who had a passion for music and felt the greatest admiration for the Saint-Cyr family, was the most generous. The endowment enabled the young man to become a priest. He was far from offended by such a requirement which brought him to love his mother even more, now adding self-pity to the pity he felt for her, but he still couldn't give shape to his recollections. Some years before his visual imagery had seemed clearer; he could see his mother as he remembered her and simultaneously see himself by her side. In time he understood that these remembrances were a late acquisition which hadn't originated in his memory. Had the reminiscence been genuine, he would have seen her alone without the young boy.

A bookworm when in the seminary he didn't run wild when he returned to Saint-Justin to spend his summer holidays there. He remained studious, pale and diligent since he had the benefit of a model, Léon Gérin, who was living in seclusion at his uncle's in the presbytery, who never went out without his notebook and who sometimes could be seen standing on the sidewalk, jotting down notes. He was then doing preliminary research for his book dealing with the rural family which is still a well-known work, one of the classics of our humble and serious literature. Armour thought him an amazing man. Gérin was his senior and he would have liked to talk to him if the occasion had presented itself. On the other hand, for want of an occasion he meant to submit to him a short novel he was writing. Unfortunately when he had finished it Gérin had already left.

He wrote the book during the summer following his *belles-lettres*. It was an action-packed adventure story. Barring minor characters, there were only two major figures, Estelle and David. Estelle loved David but he, bound by the call of duty couldn't reciprocate, although she was both bright and rich, which proved to be the death of her. As to the hero's problem, it was Armour's whose chief duty was to become a priest since his all-powerful patron Bishop Gérin kept him in college for this purpose. Estelle wasn't entirely unlike his mother so that at the outset he had brought her back to life. There's a hunting party celebrating the end of a day during which three deer have been felled. Estelle is annoyed over all this coarse, rollicking fun. She is the only girl there and she's the boss's daughter. Her father, like Mr. Grandbois or Mr. Power, had landed a number of forestry concessions thanks to dirty tricks which had best remain unmentioned here.

"Estelle looked at the lake streaked by a moonbeam. The evening entranced her so that she craved to be alone. She left her father and his coarse friends, walked to the shore, stepped into a canoe and paddled away. Her absence had gone unnoticed as each of the day's brave deeds was being retold and no one was in a hurry to bring the conversation to a close. Suddenly in the night's stillness an anguished scream echoed. All were instantly afoot.

'Someone is drowning! Let us get into the canoes! Quickly!' David said.

He had barely started off when he again heard a weak cry, a desperate call. Heading at once in the direction from which it came, paddling with all his might, he soon found himself at the scene of the accident. A capsized canoe tossed and whirled like an unfortunate wreck. Indifferent to the terrible danger involved in attempting a rescue in the midst of a whirlpool he dove and disappeared under the water like an arrow. Three times he thought he had taken hold of the victim's body and three times the force of the swirling eddy had snatched it away. His strength was at the point of failing him when, in a desperate effort his hand touched a woman's hair and with a few powerful strokes he emerged from the whirlpool clutching his burden, the imprudent Estelle. When he saw David appear, holding in his arms the limp body of his daughter, her father was beside himself. She was brought to the shore where artificial respiration was attempted. For a while Estelle remained motionless, pale, her eyes closed, seemingly unresponsive to the care being lavished upon her. At last, after approximately ten minutes the young girl opened her eyes, rose to her feet and leaning on her father's arm she slowly walked away.''

The young seminarian thought he had written a masterpiece. When it was pointed out to him that mountain lakes have no current and even fewer whirlpools he found the criticism mean and irritating. His work was far above such questions of detail and the lake had only to comply and have currents and whirlpools. He may have been right since the novel, in spite of its awkwardness, alluded to what was most personal and dear to him. Estelle rescued from the deep was soon to die, as his mother had died, as he was to die himself, suffocating, from a chest ailment. Could he retrieve her again, submerged so deeply in his memory that his mind's eye was unable to catch a glimpse of her? The rescue scene showed that he couldn't. She didn't belong to his generation. He had loved her without her knowing it and couldn't even think of meeting her again. He had only been able to conjure her up so as to lose her a second time and find her loss irrevocable.

"Time went by, pregnant with a consuming dread, punctuated by the sick girl's rending moans. At approximately twelve o'clock, her condition became critical due to the swelling of membranes obstructing the larynx. She was suffocating and struggling, throwing off her blankets, unable to tolerate anything over herself. Then, her restlessness subsided. She fell into a torpor, her breathing imperceptible enough for asphyxia to have set in..."

The pastor of Saint-Thuribe smiled weakly and said:

"I wonder how I was ever able to save Estelle from drowning. Isola, perhaps you can tell me?"

The housekeeper answered:

"You're asking too much, Father. If you'll wait for just a little while, Father Tourigny and Dr. Fauteux are going to be here any minute now. They've got enough knowledge and authority to explain it to you. Me? — If you only knew — I don't know nothing."

"They told me the novel wasn't getting me anywhere and I shouldn't persist in writing it. But what about life, Isola. Does life get you anywhere?"

"I just don't know, Father. I don't want to know."

"Life's a blind alley but you do make your way out of it all the same. You think you're caught within your own skin, your own self's captive forever. Then you get sick, recover from what you are and you're free."

The housekeeper asked Father Lupien to talk less, as the doctor had explicitly recommended.

"One more question, Isola. Are you sure that Canon Tourigny and Dr. Fauteux will come together? I thought they weren't getting along."

"Well, it seems they've cooled down since they both took the train in Batiscan to go to La Pérade and come up here. They should be in town by now, but the thaw is setting in, the roads are broken up and they must be travelling more slowly than they'd expected."

The sick man shut his eyes and seemed to have fallen asleep. The housekeeper who had been provided with an unreliable young servant-girl as a helper went down to mind her pots and pans. If she had remained in the room she would have heard him pronounce Estelle's name and then Marguerite's. She wouldn't have been offended as she thought it only natural that kind, helpful faces should appear at the bedside of a sick man on the verge of death, whether he was an ecclesiastic, a cardinal or a Pope; women's faces whose features far from being concealed by that of the Virgin rather find their unambiguous embodiment in it, even if some weren't *ladies*. Did they have unsavoury names, that of bitch or whore? That didn't make much difference as long as they were easy to deal with, kind and accommodating. When she bends over her son, who does the Virgin Mother lean on? Mary Magdalene. Whom did she lean on while Isola was in the kitchen? On Marguerite who had fiery, almond-shaped eyes and hair as strong as a horse's mane, Marguerite whom Philippe Cossette had sought out up on the Rivière des Envies so as to marry her and who didn't belong to one of the better families. She had played around with the poor assistant and yet she was the one he was calling out to. In a fever, he now remembered only the softness of her body. If Canon Tourigny had already arrived in Saint-Thuribe he would have put an end to all of this and the Virgin would have found herself bent over Father Lupien, isolated and friendless.

Exactly what had been going on in Batiscan? Simply this: although Philippe worshipped his young wife, it didn't look as if he could give her any children. She had taken it upon herself, in collusion with old Dr. Fauteux, to give him an offspring; this child she had christened Armour with a magnificent shamelessness, probably so as not to be indebted to the young ecclesiastic whose services she had appreciated and whose love she had scorned. However, far from being satisfied with the affair he had taken it very badly, thought himself guilty of a monstrous sin, unworthy of outliving it. He had eaten out of her hand and thought that she would eat out of his. So he had offended Estelle, his dim, ghostlike mother as well as gods more deep-seated, more ruthless and more implacable than his poor Jesus. He became outlandish, erratic, incoherent. Up to then Canon Tourigny had enjoyed hearing him preach but he eventually thought it necessary to forbid his going up into the pulpit. He could even conjecture, thanks to the gossip of Florence, that his assistant had been seduced by an Indian girl, but refrained from doing so out of Christian charity. The birth of Philippe's and Marguerite's son occurred in the midst of all this. He was expecting the father's visit so as to settle the date of the baptism. The father never came but went elsewhere. As we have seen, the scandalous baptism was then allowed to take place at home by the Trois-Rivières bishopric upon receipt of a medical certificate signed by Dr. Fauteux. Bishop Laflèche was in Europe and Bishop Charles-Olivier Caron had been visiting his relatives in Saint-Léon. It was thought that such an authorisation which, going against the custom of the diocese and even canon law, defied Canon Tourigny's authority, had emanated from Father Normand who expected to become a bishop one day or another, thanks to his noble bearing and because he had always been told that he would. His vanity required nothing more. He came to administer the sacrament himself. Since on that day champagne flowed rather more freely in Batiscan than it did in Trois-Rivières he had too much and returned feeling merry if not drunk in His Excellency's carriage, blessing everything in sight along the road, even the livestock. The consummation of the scandal was the name he gave the child, Father Lupien's, a name which the pastor of Batiscan would never have allowed in this instance and which astounded the assistant when he'd heard about it. He didn't come down to supper and crept outside at dusk.

"Go and fetch Father Lupien, Florence," said Canon Elias Tourigny.

He had finished eating, and having made himself comfortable in his armchair, he had just lit the cigar he usually smoked each evening. His indignation against Father Normand, the Cossettes, as well as Dr. Fauteux hadn't even shown. An evening like all other evenings had apparently just begun. However Florence didn't seem anxious to go up.

"Did you hear me, Florence? My assistant and I have some talking to do, and it's important."

The housekeeper went up the stairs and came down saying that Father Lupien wasn't in his room.

"He must have gone out for some fresh air. You can go back to work now. I will see him when he comes in."

The canon seemed to be enjoying his cigar. Florence knew that he was in fact far from feeling the unruffled coolness he displayed because she had known him for so long. She went towards the kitchen thinking:

"Well, there's a man who's in the saddle for you."

She felt reassured, even if the *curé* hadn't got over his apprehensions at all knowing that his assistant was God-knows-where, in the dark, obsessed with the desire to put an end to himself.

Isola wasn't coming back up. The young priest moaned, but so feebly that it could only have been meant for himself and God. He found it difficult to breathe, couldn't get enough air into his lungs. If he wanted more the pain kept him from breathing in.

"Marguerite, what have you made of me? I didn't know what you were looking for. You took me in and drove me out as if I'd been a dog. If you just knew how awful I feel you wouldn't be hovering above me like a star. You would come down and put your hand on my forehead. Do it. Now, Marguerite. Before Canon Tourigny comes in. He has already saved me from you once and he would do it all over again."

70

"I only wanted a child from you, Armour. You gave it to me in short order and I couldn't keep you. I had a jealous husband and you had a jealous *curé* yourself and we weren't going to run off into the bush, were we? Besides, another Armour had replaced you and I loved him with all my heart. Would you have wanted me to give him up for your sake?"

"No. You must love him, mend through him the web of days which had been torn in me. I was only a stray dog dragging his rope along, a rope which a ghostlike woman had begun to braid."

"Don't denigrate the poor, young girl. I could only catch hold of you thanks to that rope, you tramp, you savage."

And Marguerite's hand rested on his forehead. He had taken his fill of what little air he could breathe and was sleeping when Isola came back up from the kitchen.

"Sweet God," she prayed, "make him recover."

Canon Tourigny and Dr. Fauteux driven by the owner of a sleigh they had rented in Sainte-Anne-de-la-Pérade were plodding towards Saint-Thuribe. A big draught horse inured to human harshness still was the animal best suited to the road which was virtually impassable.

"What can you do for a man you've already saved from death?"

"It's a question of the individual you're dealing with. Some would be callous enough to enjoy being saved three times a week."

"He hangs in there."

Dr. Fauteux didn't answer.

"Don't you have anything to say to that, doctor?"

"He hangs in there. How can you know that? There are so many loudmouths who make a name

71

for themselves as men who hang in there. Besides, let me tell you that I'm no theologian and I don't care for generalities.''

Feeling dissatisfied with himself the doctor added:

''One shouldn't be simple-minded about these things: who can claim that he has saved another man from death? You might answer that it's a fact. But nothing proves to me that another man might not have done just as much.''

CHAPTER 7

In time, the practice of medicine which had at first made him uneasy, apprehensive and often miserable had turned Dr. Fauteux into a devious person; he avoided coming out into the open so that he could see without being seen, speculate as to the desires and intentions of those who consulted him without betraying his own. Even if he ran the risk of seeming obscure to them, he was particularly reticent with the young who no doubt had many good points, who were more precocious than he himself had been, but whom he found too numerous. A man has a quota of individuals who belong to his own species, his own tribe, with whom he can enter into an easygoing, natural and reciprocal relationship. He had exceeded his and day after day had to meet strangers with whom he had no desire to be acquainted. He had learned to lie without hesitation, inventing diseases which were easily understandable to these newcomers, which enlightened them as to their case and cheered them up, since they involved treatment and recovery. They were fictitious creations of the mind, adapted to theirs. They were sold at their market value and he only accepted reasonable fees. He sometimes reproached himself for not raising them since his patients would then have prized his fictions even more, as they would have provided both relief and flattery. Patients who did him the honor of consulting him were coming in greater numbers ever since he had stopped fretting and had put paid to his sensitivity and wretchedness over the ills resulting from a lifestyle, a certain kind of society, the school, the family, and which no one asked him to change. These fictitious ailments comprehended all possible evils, even the one which originates in the fact of being alive, which he occasionally noticed without trying to express it in clear terms however, either through intellectual sluggishness or because of the patient's refusal to hear it mentioned.

"Canon Tourigny, I'm not a defender of truth like you. More often than not illness complies with social convention. It must be conceptualized first, which allows you to put the case clearly and have the patient recover according to the laws of logic. And there's medical procedure for you. You recover in much the same way as you get on the sick list, after a preliminary statement."

"Doctor, aren't you making too much of the tricks of the trade? For example didn't you say, basing your estimate on the diagnosis of your colleague from Sainte-Anne, that we didn't have to hurry since the patient's condition comes to a head only nine days after the outbreak of pneumonia?"

"Pneumonia ain't no joke," said Bessette, the most reliable of Sainte-Anne's coachmen. His backside was beginning to feel sore. He was alone on the board which he used as a seat and behind which both notables weren't just taking their ease but talking to each other like Englishmen in incomprehensible French he couldn't make out. He wasn't unaware of the respect he owed them since he had a bishop in the family himself, Bishop Gérard Bessette who headed a diocese in Ontario. At least his eminent cousin had enough sense to keep his trap shut, his jaws clamped tight as if he had a toad in his mouth. But these people, the canon and the doctor who between them didn't even amount to a bishop, never stopped talking, or rather never stopped pretending to talk. With his Mignonne ploughing down the road between Sainte-Anne and Saint-Thuribe, the snow coming up to her belly, Bessette would eventually have felt very lonely indeed.

Dr. Fauteux ignoring the coachman's remark answered Canon Tourigny:

"Yes, we do have a few minor certainties but what are they? Exceptions confirming the rule. Unfortunately some colleagues base their practice on them, like this man from Sainte-Anne whom I trust whenever he comes across as typical an illness as straightforward, acute, right lobular pneumonia. But that's exceptional. Most patients don't suffer from a definite complaint. What will my colleague do then? He will either force them to be sick according to due process like Thomas Diafoirus[1] or deny them the right to be ill, especially if they can't afford to pay him. In both cases, certainly in the majority of cases, he's raving."

"He might be proven right in the long run."

"In the meantime he is less happy than a bone-setter and becoming comparatively more dangerous. The long run! One day the main benefit reaped from the acquisition of medical knowledge will be the

---

[1] Thomas Diafoirus: a defender of orthodox Aristotelian medical practice in Molière's *Le malade imaginaire* (1673).

ability to protect oneself against the profession.''

This made the canon laugh as well as the coachman who had gotten the point now.

''So, you're an absolute sceptic, an unbeliever even as far as medicine is concerned.''

''The survival of the species is ensured and medicine will be outlawed, eventually. Its only purpose is to keep old sores going. As to restoring one's patients to health and saving lives, that's absurd. Why, do we even have the right to do it?''

Dr. Fauteux seemed to be angry and Bessette was beginning to enjoy the ride. He had always heard of Dr. Fauteux as an old practical joker who would challenge a man's convictions so as to earn his trust. He thought the doctor wanted to provoke Canon Tourigny but he canon was nobody's fool.

''Then, why do you do it?''

''There was a time when human beings were scarce and one couldn't be sure that the species would survive. I do it out of force of habit and because I enjoy practising medicine.''

''Words, words, words,'' thought the coachman who figured the canon's answer had clinched it. He got down from the sleigh under the pretext of checking his horse's harness and when he stood near the collar, out of sight of his distinguished clients, he took a flask of whiskey out of his overcoat.

''Here's to you, Mignonne.'' Then he climbed back into the sleigh thinking that everything was just dandy. Dr. Fauteux had taken advantage of the fact that the coachman was standing off to ask the canon just whose life he had saved.

''Your assistant's? After a baptism celebrated behind your back in a house near a bridge? Well, Father Normand is cocky, looks dignified, has no brains at all and indulges in the inveterate habit of already considering himself a bishop. It mustn't have been too hard to take him for a ride.''

''You were a party to that, doctor.''

''Even more than you would expect. Are you referring to my medical certificate which said that the child's health didn't allow him to be baptized in church?''

''Yes. They showed it to me at the episcopal palace.''

''That's nothing. Did you know I'd previously brought Father Lupien to Marguerite's notice?''

''You did?''

''She wanted to have a son.''

''I know. She had me celebrate nine masses in Sainte-Marguerite.''

''I thought that Philippe just couldn't give her one even if he seemed to have a rugged constitution. No doubt, you were also aware of this: as long as his good mother was alive every servant girl in the house found him a devil with the ladies and there was no other inconvenience than the sin itself. So you can understand that your poor little Sainte-Marguerite, virgin and martyr, wasn't much use. Mind you, I'd been told of the novena and hadn't advised against it.''

''Should I thank you for not having done so?''

''I really can't see why, Father.''

''I suppose you then took the matter in hand.''

''Tell me now, who do you think could drop in at the Cossette residence when Philippe was absent more often that not, without anyone taking exception to it? Your curate and myself.''

''And yourself. Your forefather was named Faustus...''

"Your assistant's name, on the other hand, was Armour and the word's consonance wasn't thought disagreeable. Moreover his age was more in keeping with Mrs. Cossette's than mine."

"And yet, Faust can grow young again when it's a question of pleasing Marguerite, can't he?"

The doctor began to laugh.

"Oh!" he said, "if I only could have! But how? Mephisto doesn't seem to appreciate the charm of the Trois-Rivières diocese or of your parish. No matter how we invoked him he never showed up and as far as Marguerite was concerned, Father Lupien had no rival to contend with. I wasn't jealous. I liked them both and felt I was a party to their love-making out of sympathy for them. I was touched. Why just think of it, I'd never been a pimp before."

"You went and did that!"

"More than that: I insisted that she should display her gratefulness to your assistant by naming her son Armour."

The pastor, justifiably indignant, told Dr. Fauteux he had misjudged him but that from now on he would consider him an evil and vicious individual. Bessette, the coachman, trying to tone down a quarrel which confused him since he respected and admired both men, turned around to offer them some whiskey.

"You'll feel better."

Both notables refused. Before corking the flask he had a good, stiff drink. Dr. Fauteux said to him:

"Bessette, if you see any little white mice, grab a couple for the reverend."

"If you see any black rats give them to the doctor."

"By the way," Dr. Fauteux resumed, "nothing keeps you from declaring in the pulpit next Sunday that I am the man you claim, an evil and vicious individual, a kind of huge black rat. I even wonder if by refraining from doing so you wouldn't be coming to terms with the forces of evil.''

Father Tourigny didn't answer just then. Turning to the coachman he told him that he had changed his mind, took a mouthful of whiskey, handed the flask to the doctor who did the same, then handed it back to Bessette who thanked them kindly.

The whiskey may have helped the canon bear in mind that he was a powerful man and that his authority, although God-given, was also due to his good services rendered to the parish.

''Denounce you from the pulpit? Doctor, you have me worried. Do you actually think I'm insane?''

He was already less cross, still offended but no longer angry.

''We have too many mutual friends to discriminate between yours and mine. God doesn't require one to separate the wheat from the chaff, probably because there is some of both, right and left, in you and in me. But getting back to human nature, that blend of milk and fury, blood and tenderness, since you have loved this spirited girl from up-river, that's another story.''

''Love isn't the right word.''

''How do you know? Age is nothing but a mask. At heart childhood and youth are a man's only vital and genuine self.

''You might say that I wanted to help her out.''

''Why didn't you say so? Bearing in mind your convictions, and God knows that you have hardly any, you acted for the best.''

The doctor answered proudly.

''I achieved what I set out to do.''

"You had taken everything into account but the victim. On the night of the notorious baptism Father Lupien didn't come down to supper. After all he was entitled to fast; but later on, during the evening, when I sent Florence to fetch him, his room was empty. He had vanished and was wandering in the dark trying to do himself in. I immediately suspected what was going on but how could I put a stop to it? How could I prevent the water from drifting by at the end of the pier?"

"What did you do?"

"I kept on smoking my cigar, taking my time, and no longer felt apprehensive about the river. I thought that he was too ashamed to come out into the open and that when he had left the presbytery he must have gone to hide in the barn of the church vestry where, as it happened, a beggar had hanged himself some years before."

"I remember," the coachman said. "He was always bitching about something or other. The name was Trudeau. He came from farther off than Laprairie and was headed for the States. I knew him well. Having a lot of money might have cheered him up some. He couldn't beg properly because a man has to have a way with him and be smart to beg. All he could do was scare hell out of everybody. He was right to bitch and I think he was right to hang himself too. There are three big beams going across the barn, you know, and one end of the hay-fork rope is tied to the beam in the center. All you have to do is untie it from the fork and climb up on the loft with it, tie your slip-knot, jump and you're hanging."

"Mister Bessette," said Canon Tourigny, "you seem to be an expert on the subject but don't go

80

and think that Father Lupien tried to imitate the beggar.''

"He didn't? Then everybody has another guess coming, just like when we all figure that he's the father of little Mithridates, Armour Cossette. Look, we all know and we all shut up. What more can you ask? You're not going to organize a great big retreat and preach to us about lies and liars. You see, the main thing is that the kids don't find out.''

"You're right, Bessette. I even wonder whether you wouldn't have been a better canon than I.''

"Canon Tourigny, you aren't like most ecclesiastics. That's why I'll say you might have become as good a coachman as I am.''

Bessette hummed a tune between his teeth. He finally belonged even if he was sitting alone in front of the big sleigh on an uncomfortable board. Speaking about the beggar, Canon Tourigny had told Father Lupien:

"Hanged. I suppose it's out of our bailiwick now. His pastor is the one who should be asking himself some questions. Was it insanity, a protest against some injustice committed by the clergy? A man's motive for hanging himself in the barn of a church vestry may not be the same as for doing it in a farmer's barn.''

Father Lupien had replied:

"We must bear in mind that black sun whose icy rays are keener than the other's, reaching down to the soul's depths and making life before God and man unendurable.''

Was he speaking of the torpor of depression, the despair of a body deprived of vitality? The canon hadn't dared to ask. He had declared that, in short, there wasn't much one could find out about a poor man who had hanged himself, blue all over, his swollen tongue sticking out between his teeth.

"Any question you could ask would be academic. He will ultimately be damned to the satisfaction of all the earth's sinners, buried in a jiffy in the potter's field, like Judas, as if he had betrayed Christ.

"Is that the way a case like this should be handled?" Father Lupien had asked, suddenly very concerned.

"I'm not that sure. You abide by the requirements of canon law and proceed, harshly, without prayer or ceremony against a poor wretch, confused by the pity you feel and don't dare show. You try to find a way of interceding with Our Lady, the Virgin Mary, and you can't because there may be none. And the black sun you spoke of — which I couldn't imagine at first — that sun shines with a blazing fire to obscure your quest and keep you from reaching a helpful Mother. You remain alone, besmirched by such a dreadful calamity."

The assistant had begun to laugh hysterically.

"And to think that you are said to be nothing more than a man who likes horses."

In fact, few people from Trois-Rivières to Grondines and in the inland parishes could brag they had outrun the *curé* of Batiscan's carriage.

"How did you answer him?" asked Dr. Fauteux.

"I answered that what people said was probably true, because it is true. I like horses and make no secret of it. We are commanded to love and you've got to start somewhere which doesn't mean that one has to confine oneself to the stable."

The canon hesitated.

"I can't recall exactly... I must have added that we were all Christians, that without our Lord's sacrifice for the salvation of the world I wouldn't have been able to bear the sight of animals, and not only animals, men too, being battered about, slaughtered and shrieking about death on this earth."

"In other words, thanks to Christ you no longer find all these cries of agony offensive."

"This is incomprehensible to you, doctor, but God has transcended death so as to make it a greater life still."

The doctor granted that the canon and himself disagreed fundamentally.

"Which is regrettable all the same because we would have gotten along fine otherwise. So, I became a party to the defence of Marguerite's interests and you were... Exactly what happened when you had guessed that the poor man was in the church vestry barn?"

"Father Lupien is all thumbs when it's a question of putting something into practice you know and he has no imagination at all. I finished my cigar. Since he was going to emulate the beggar it was a question of getting my hands on a good knife and turning up in the barn neither too early nor too late. But as always happens in these cases one tends to show up ahead of time, which I did, unobtrusively. I only had to wait for him to jump to cut the rope at once. He found himself sitting on the floor between the two haylofts, his slipknot still hanging about his neck, stunned. I'd rushed at him to slacken the knot and I was holding the large, red-handled knife in my right hand. He was even more bewildered when he heard me say:

"Mister, I'm going to kill you. Look at this knife."

"I don't like the looks of the handle much," he said.

"You'll like the blade better. Besides don't worry about a thing. I take full responsibility for the sin so you can die, just like you want to, without being damned."

"What did he do?" the doctor asked.

"He's no fool. He'd figured me out and he smiled at me like a child. 'Come,' I told him, taking him by the arm, 'you have been appointed pastor of Saint-Thuribe. I will take you there no later than tomorrow.' Florence could tell that I hadn't gone out for nothing and the supper which Father Lupien had done without was awaiting him on the table. He ate heartily and we went up to bed at the usual time. On the next day I was travelling to Trois-Rivières where, coincidentally, His Excellency Charles-Olivier Caron happened to have returned the day before, in time to see Father Normand in the bishop's carriage, cold sober, even if he still granted blessings all round. Getting my point across was no problem and the Normand family got up a subscription so as to ship its abbot to Europe where he could restore his episcopal dignity. The pastor of Saint-Thuribe was summoned back to the bishop's palace. So when I returned to Batiscan I could take Father Lupien to his new parish whose former incumbent hadn't moved out yet. He was stumbling all over his furniture, hampered by his housemaid, a decent sort of woman called Isola, who wanted to come along with him. I would say that I straightened things out fairly well. I began by convincing the man who was a nice fellow but still something of a country yokel to bring along only a small suitcase since, as I said, one should travel light down a road leading to honors. He didn't care for honors at all. I mentioned his duty. He finally followed me out carrying two suitcases, surrendering the furniture and the housekeeper to Father Lupien."

The big sleigh drawn by Mignonne, a sturdy mare who had been through worse, kept on ploughing down the road. The coachman, turning towards both passengers gave them the welcome news that in less than an hour they would reach their destination, the presbytery courtyard.

"Your mare didn't hurt her legs too badly?" asked Canon Tourigny.

"She's much too smart to do that," answered the coachman. "Just think, Father, she knew the days when Big Boss Wilbrod was still around — that bloody jobber who didn't mind having his men worked to death and his horses bruised up on the Rivière Sainte-Anne. Got what was coming to him when he died, too."

"He drowned. It was an accident."

Doctor Fauteux was better acquainted with the facts of the case.

"That's an unfounded supposition," he said, "but the bush is so dense there they couldn't even have brought charges against a pine tree or a spruce. Besides, the rocks of the Rivière Sainte-Anne are sharp enough for no one to have minded his head looking like it had been bashed in with an axe."

The coachman thought enough had been said about a case in which Canon Tourigny wasn't unduly interested; the incident had occurred way off, outside the boundaries of his parish. However, the canon believed he should remind Dr. Fauteux that there was no such thing as an accident. One only spoke of accidents to dodge divine justice.

"Coming back to Father Lupien, Canon Tourigny, you certainly helped him out. I was more or less aware of the fact and I wasn't annoyed. We had done him in and I felt I'd been a bit irresponsible. His son is a beautiful child. I'm sure he'll grow into a fine, powerful man, the second member of a dynasty consecrated from your own pulpit, as you may remember."

"And how! Father Lupien even got next to this girl because I... Well. I thought I was sending him to apologize and was in fact leading him into temptation. I ought to have known better but you can't surpervise everything in a parish even if you've the most permanent status. Fate takes advantage of this to play tricks on you. Heading for Saint-Thuribe with you, doctor, I do feel somewhat as if I was making my way back to the church vestry barn."

"Except that you're doing it with me and there'll be no hayfork rope. Yet, this illness is suffocating him and I don't have a cure as efficient as the large red-handled knife you were holding in your right hand the first time."

"I also wonder whether we have the right to keep men from dying against their will."

Yes Father, of course we do. At the time, their will is nothing more than a stray impulse. Besides, this is quite different. I'm absolutely sure now that this young ecclesiastic who is about to become a professor of Letters, an excellent one, and he knows it, doesn't feel like dying at all. He will live if he wants to, just like he wouldn't have given you half a chance of saving him if he'd really wanted to kill himself."

They were just driving into the village of Saint-Thuribe. Dr. Fauteux added:

"He will probably enjoy your presence more than mine."

Canon Tourigny turned towards the doctor with an angry look and reminded him that he hadn't come to please Father Lupien but to look after him.

"Isn't your name Faustus? Didn't your forefather wear the uniform of Prince Frederick?"

"He was also insane as you may know. But so what if my name is Faustus or Fauteux? Does that make any difference? What are you driving at?"

"I wouldn't hesitate to make use of the devil if he promised me to get Father Lupien back on his feet. That's what I'm driving at."

Dr. Fauteux asked his fellow traveller whether he was acquainted with the story of Faust and Marguerite — very well known because of the opera. The canon had heard of it, more or less.

"First, let me tell you that it's old Dr. Faust who, in exchange for his soul, recovers his youth and seduces Marguerite while she, far from being better off for it, doesn't survive her disgrace. If you want to draw a parallel, you should acknowledge the fact that I haven't gotten any younger, while in her big home near the toll-bridge Marguerite Cossette is more beautiful and happier than she ever was."

"We may get distorted versions of stories from the old country which are merely confusing to us," the canon admitted.

"There's a devil called Mephisto in the original version. He's missing in ours. On the other hand, we've got your curate who can't be found in the original. My grandfather's name may have been Faustus, but you remind me of this as if I'd had a hand

87

in it. What's more, I have the impression you're confusing him with Mephisto. Besides how could you explain the absurd intrusion of Mithridates in the story of Faust and Marguerite? Because Mithridates was king of Pontus while Philippe owns the tollbridge? Some hodgepodge. And you're dishing it out to me in Saint-Thuribe whose pastor suffers from pneumonia, as if that isn't enough. Look, if you brought me along to cure him, stop the foolishness.''

The canon thankèd Dr. Fauteux.

''Your common sense restores my confidence.''

''You know I'll do all I can.''

Father Lupien died on April 25, 1873. He would have been thirty-six in July. On the morning of his death, the ninth day of his illness, the critical day on which opposed forces clashed openly, the day which could just as well have been that of his recovery, the canon and the doctor were looking out the kitchen window after breakfast searching for a favorable omen in the presbytery yard. There were some chaffinches and grosbeaks only passing through, not in much of a hurry, headed for their spring meeting-point up north. On a willow branch a blue jay which hadn't migrated for the winter was shrieking at the intruders. Behind the church vestry barn, on the manure heap, the crows had plenty to say to each other judging from the racket they raised.

''The crows are a long way off,'' said the canon.

''You think so?''

''I mean they're out of sight. I wouldn't like to see them in the courtyard.''

''My dear canon, you are more superstitious than a pagan.''

Three blackbirds, their eyes flashing, three magnificent and fearful looking males landed in the courtyard and began walking, jerky, soldierlike, towards the good guys who flew off one after the other.

"I think we had better go up," the doctor said.

Isola, weeping, was all they could hear.

Behind a portrait of the deceased a quotation from Father Armour Lupien had been written:

It is the Father who proceeds from the
Son and without the death of Jesus on Calvary
there would be no God.

It wasn't noticed by anyone except Dr. Fauteux.

"Who is it by?" he asked Canon Tourigny, who remembered how sorry he had been whenever the young priest was preaching and he could see the doctor's pew near the main aisle empty as usual.

"It was one of Father Lupien's favourite themes. I find it somewhat paradoxical and even, perhaps, heretical. That's why the quotation isn't signed. Whenever he preached on the subject I glanced at your pew and regretted your not being there."

"It's my turn to do so now. He was high-spirited, had a capacity for original thought, flashes of insight. I certainly could have helped him more than I did. Marguerite knew him in a different light and I was only acquainted with him through her. I was Mephisto after all. He turned out to be an embodiment of the rejuvenated Dr. Faust. I don't think I'll be able to forgive myself."

Some weeks later, the old doctor was discovered hanging by the neck in the church vestry barn. A sheet of paper was also found on which he had written:

At long last a prominent citizen, a man who knows
what he is doing goes and joins the insane and
the lost in potter's field.

CHAPTER 8

On the morning of Dr. Fauteux' funeral the weather was unsettled. No dew had fallen and it looked like it might rain during the ceremony. For the first time in his life Canon Tourigny was angered against God and said to him:

"Listen! Send me a single drop and I won't hang myself in the barn, I'll do it in church. My testament will be an ordinance forbidding the people of this parish to honor you and prescribing that they never set foot in your church again."

The overcast was low and on the verge of dissolving into rain to the point where at the river's mouth the three masts of *The Saint Elias* were barely visible. The great windjammer had just sailed back from a long and difficult voyage. It had reached Senegal on the African continent, Senegal whose capital was Saint-Louis at the time and whose inhabitants called themselves Kanadien. Interminable palavering ensued after which a huge idol had been offered to these other *Canadiens* who had come from beyond the seas. It was a squatting female figure, flat-faced with oversized ears as well as an open mouth displaying a set of long teeth. The idol had no admirers among the crew which thought it only suitable to scare hell out of the kids.

"What can I possibly do with that?" Philippe Cossette alias Mithridates had asked.

"Whatever you want. All we can say is this idol was offered to us by people we certainly didn't care to offend."

Marguerite had thought of putting it in her garden at the back of the house. But, meanwhile, Dr. Fauteux had killed himself and the canon claimed the idol. Philippe was glad to hand it over.

"You want to burn it, don't you."

"No. Get it up to the cemetery. It will stand in the potter's field, over the grave of our poor friend."

Since he couldn't provide the doctor with the proper funeral he had promised him, Canon Tourigny had prepared a remarkable ritual as a mark of the respect and compassion he felt. Since he couldn't use the church he had declared that it would remain closed on that day. Since canon law forbade him to ring the bells so as to give public notice that the funeral was being held, he ordered them to ring all night and in Batiscan they tolled all night long. At daybreak, the canon silenced them and ordered his sexton to put up the great stand on the church steps surrounded by six tall golden candlesticks.

"What if it rains, Reverend?"

"Hector-Marie, keep your guesswork to yourself and do what I say. Then go and tell the good old biddies and the pensioners that if I have no right to say mass for François Fauteux's soul to rest in peace I won't celebrate it for theirs either."

It was then that Canon Tourigny who, on his own initiative was doing more than was required of him and was doing it with a cold-blooded determination, had warned God to delay his rainfall.

"I don't like that fog trailing along the dry ground under billowing clouds. I'm not asking for sunshine. Under the circumstances a gloomy day will do even better as long as you don't send me a shower or a downpour which would ruin my ritual."

Well, God considered himself forewarned. He scattered his rain on the neighboring villages, but it only began falling in Batiscan after noontime had gone by without an Angelus, when those who attended the service had already returned home. This is the way things went: at eight, the people who came from the village, the parish and other parishes even, had already begun to arrive. They came because Dr. Fauteux, though an unbeliever who scoffed at the medical profession, had always taken very good care of his patients. Everyone was aware of this and in spite of his tragic death all thought that he had earned public recognition. Although the weather seemed to be taking a turn for the worse, an even greater number of people were there because they wanted to see how Canon Tourigny would pay tribute to his old friend; and when they did, they were beside themselves with admiration. The large catafalque was already set up on the church steps when the first of them arrived. Some wanted to go in and were told that they could always try:

"The bells have been tolling all night long and are silent now. They will not ring for the Angelus and there won't be a mass since a requiem mass can't be celebrated for the doctor."

Sceptics tried to open the doors which didn't even budge. They realized the doors had been bolted.

"What if it rains?"

"My pastor, Canon Elias Tourigny," answered Hector-Marie, "will have you know that no one is forcing you to stay here and you can all go back home.''

Hector-Marie had donned his uniform. Naturally he spoke with an angry look, staring at the man he was talking to as if he considered him guilty of all the sins of the earth. Soon enough, as the crowd gradually got bigger no one wanted to come and try the doors or mention rain any more. The church choir, a large one, reputedly one of the best in the diocese, had gotten into position on both sides of the bier, while two rows of altar boys stood on the church steps. Soon, the canon appeared before the bier, wearing his sacerdotal garb. For a moment the magnificence of his vestments kept everyone from noticing a detail which was entirely unexpected. Around his neck he wore a rope, the rope Dr. Fauteux had used to hang himself. Then a confused murmur spread among the crowd, gradually growing into a vast moan and a voice singing solo, a woman's voice, broke into the *Dies Irae*. A second voice responded to it and a third and finally the chorus as a whole sang the awe-inspiring hymn.

Suddenly, Canon Tourigny kneeled. He had just seen the processional cross held by his new assistant and before which the crowd moved aside. The coffin followed it carried by six colleagues of the deceased. Then, walking alone, bravely, a very young boy nicknamed Mithridates II. He was Armour Cossette, the doctor's godson, accompanied by his parents Philippe and Marguerite, who followed him at a distance — the first, powerful and feared, the second, more beautiful than ever. After them came a number of ecclesiastics, pastors and assistants from east of the Saint-Maurice, from Sainte-Flore, Grand-Mère from Cap-de-la-Madeleine, all the way to Saint-Prosper and

94

Grondines. By taking part in the procession they showed that they were attending the service as dignitaries of a province of their country and not as representatives of religious authority which was shouldered by a single man, the one who was kneeling and remained so until the six doctors had come up to him. He then rose so as to let them slide the coffin onto the platform. The choir was silent. The doctors withdrew and the choir boys brought the holy water and incense. The canon proceeded with the Libera as usual then handed back their utensils to the choir boys and walked towards the main door of the church which he tested — it was locked — on which he knocked, lightly at first with the joint of his right forefinger, then banging it with both his fists. At the same time a baritone voice was singing: "Knock and it shall be opened unto you." The crowd then clearly heard these words of Joe Magloire, a big red-haired man whose wife had been saved by the doctor twice as the story went and who, in any case, thought that she had.

"Christ! We'll batter the God-damned door down!"

Some of the biggest men in the parish, among them Philippe Cossette, stepped forward. The canon stopped banging and sent his sexton to tell Magloire and Cossette to stay put. All the ecclesiastics present then realized the dangers involved in the improvisation of ritual. The voice which had been singing solo, the woman's voice heard previously, rose at once so keen, so high, so powerful and so faint that all could hear it while in their heart all feared that it would break.

"My Lord! My Lord!" said the voice, "If I have knocked and you have not answered, then your house is empty and you are among us."

The parish priest of Sainte-Flore turned towards his colleague from Saint-Tite and both looked at each other lost in admiration as both had formerly been the canon's assistants. They were amazed at this masterly capacity for breaking new ground and yet taking everything into account. The canon had kneeled again before the bier. The voice kept on singing and the word was out in the crowd:

"That's Mrs. Saint-Louis from Machiche. When she sings and she's moved, her throat swells like a dove's."

"My Lord! My Lord! you are here among us but why did you abandon the one we loved, the man with whose assistance we came into the world, lived and died, whose left hand did not know all of the wealth his right hand gave? Lord, why cut him off from us, why leave him isolated, crucified to his own self under the unbearable rays of the black sun? Why did you allow him to take his own life when he had given life to so many?"

This sums up what the high, flawless, barely modulated voice sang. It was a lament, in fact. All saw Canon Tourigny kneeling, the rope about his neck, and knew that this lament was first and foremost his own. When it had come to an end he bowed deeply before the coffin. He may even possibly have kissed the ground as was the custom in the East in the days of Jehovah and his prophets. Then he rose and turned towards the onlookers. There were so many that he felt anxious since his voice didn't carry far and he deliberately wanted all to hear him. He hadn't noticed that the low-lying clouds as well as a slight wind blowing towards the river would help. He spoke slowly, making each word he said stand out and heard by all, even by a group which stood on the pier.

"I never knew how to speak to begin with. I never had the eloquence of the apostles and was more of a horseman than a man of God and many here are aware of it, because they said so."

"Yeah, Christalmighty! I said it!" yelled Joe, "but listen, all of you. I lied."

"The Lord will be grateful to you, Joe, for putting some heart into me."

"It's the truth!"

"The truth is that I wear a dreadful rope around my neck. The truth is it's choking me."

Magloire, out of Irish candor wanted to butt in again but realized that he had been surrounded by Philippe Cossette's best men.

"C'mon now Joe, you're not going to keep a man of God from talking?"

He agreed and apologized.

"The doctor was the nicest guy I ever met."

"Sure Joe, but look behind you. There's a crowd going right back to the pier. Don't you know there's never been anything like this service?"

"Lord," Canon Tourigny went on, "you have stepped out of your church to walk among us as the spirit of unity and mutual understanding. Grant that I may be able to speak to the people of my parish as well as to all of those who came from far and wide, whose presence honors the memory of my poor friend. His body lies under this catafalque and I will have to bury him in the potter's field without taking it into church. But even if he had been the best of Catholics, if he'd died drowning in a lake of holy water, he wouldn't have been more fortunate and would have gone directly from his residence to his cemetery lot because today this church will remain empty. There will be no Angelus, there will be no mass, there will be no divine presence. On my authority as the pastor of Batiscan I have decided that God would go for a breath of fresh air, even if the day isn't all one could wish for with its overcast sky and the fog rolling in the yardarms of our three-master and of our schooners anchored at the river's mouth. I have come to this decision so that He might pay his last respects along with us to a doctor who may have passed for an unbeliever, whom I haven't often seen sitting in his pew near the church's main aisle, who fought the autocracy of Bishop Laflèche but who may have been more of a Christian than one would think. When Christ, who didn't care much for hierarchies, who didn't pick his friends but took them as he found them, who would probably have put up at the hotel rather than at the presbytery if he'd ever come down here; when Christ took upon himself the sins of all mankind he didn't pick the best way of acquiring a good reputation and didn't die crucified between two convicts for nothing. If he hadn't been a Christian, François Fauteux would have come into the church first so as to join his devoted wife in consecrated ground. There are six pallbearers standing before me here, six of his colleagues who are in a position to determine his merit, to make a value judgment on the services rendered to the population for such a long time and not one, not a single one, I say, would have declined to write "death by strangulation due to temporary insanity" on the death certificate, at my request. They could have thought it possible. Why shouldn't they give the benefit of the doubt to an unfortunate colleague? They didn't do it because Dr. Fauteux, under the influence of a depression which had exhausted him, considered himself guilty of everything he was probably not responsible for. He left the following note:

At long last, I, Jean-François Fauteux — gentleman, doctor of medicine — in full possession of my faculties and conscious of the consequences of my act, bring my life to an end and insist on joining the insane and the lost in the potter's field.

I can't judge him. I have no right to judge him. I cannot find it in my heart to judge him. I have done all that I had to do. I act according to the last will and testament of my life-long friend and we will now take him to the place of infamy. And yet I don't consider him dishonored. Because he thought of those whose companion he will be from now on, because he wanted to be shut in with them under the earth. My brethren, my children, listen to what I am telling you: was his crime such a great one since, from this day onwards, there will be less infamy in our village?''

This is what Canon Elias Tourigny said. Although he had been addressing a huge audience everyone had understood. Most wept, silently, unself-consciously, because they had just witnessed something beautiful. The pallbearers marched up to take hold of the coffin. This time, the canon himself walked before them carrying the great cross. The church was surrounded on three sides by the cemetery and the potter's field lay at the back, concealed by a monumental Calvary scene, which suggested that the parish wasn't one of the poorest in the diocese. The procession turned to the right and everyone soon understood why. The canon kneeled in the pathway, still holding the cross high. The six doctors did the same after having laid the casket down on the ground. On a tombstone whose upper part was a statue of the Virgin these words were engraved:

Here lies
Marie-Josephte Trudel
wife of
Dr. François Fauteux

No one dared to speak since this pause meant that the couple which had often been separated in the course of a lifetime would remain so after death. The memory of the young woman was evoked in the minds of those who had known her, inconspicuous and discreet, sitting alone in the family's pew every Sunday. When her husband was busy elsewhere she would take patients in with the greatest possible civility. She was without a doubt the best educated, the most unpretentious woman in Batiscan. When almost fifty she was still referred to as the doctor's young wife. Her death had been sudden and the doctor who was ten years her senior had never gotten over her loss. Even the thought of a second marriage seemed intolerable to him.

When the canon rose, and the pallbearers getting ready to follow him, did the same, a woman screamed. It was Marguerite Cossette, whose husband couldn't control her. A number of people had to take her home and she was still struggling, going at them tooth and claw like a tigress. Her son walked on, bravely following his godfather's coffin. But when the procession had passed round the Calvary and arrived in the potter's field where a grave awaited it, he caught sight of the tall Senegalese idol, squatting, its size out of all proportion to its lower limbs, its bulging breasts with nipples bigger than a cow's dugs, its long-drawn ears, flat face, gaping mouth armed with a terrifying set of teeth, and he understood that the potter's field was adjacent to hell, the kingdom of horrors. He was too young to say a word. He saw the rest of the ritual through, saw the coffin go down into the grave, heard the noise of the earth being thrown on it. When the grave had been filled, the gravediggers trampled the ground with their boots and then placed the monstrous idol which must have been carved out of a light, soft wood over the man who had been his godfather, a kind of granddaddy. It was all over now. The canon as well as the doctors were already moving off. Alone, Armour Cossette alias Mithridates II stood there.

"Go home, kid," one of the gravediggers said.

Those who came to look the idol over also told him to leave, but it wasn't any use. Someone thought of notifying the canon who came as quickly as he could, almost running and picked the child up in his arms. Although until then he had been able to keep his self-control, he now burst into tears.

"Armour," he said, "Armour, my boy."

The lad felt himself going to pieces and began to cry.

"Stop that. Stop it! Cut it out. A man shouldn't cry. Ever."

"You think you're not crying?"

"It isn't the same thing. I cry for joy. You're just like your father. If you only knew."

CHAPTER 9

After the doctor's death, Canon Tourigny who, until then had been the most home-loving of parish priests began calling at the Mithridates residence by the bridge. On the occasion of his second visit he was very surprised to hear Marguerite say

Forsaken by Caesar, Christ is my salvation
Hope's star gleaming o'er frustrated expectations.

It was embarrassing. The verses were by Rotrou, she said, and the magnificent creature went on to quote two more, describing a fight to the finish.

Renouncing life itself in so sacred a trust
Be lavish of thy blood though you bring dust to dust.

"Mrs. Cossette, you certainly can quote poetry well. Now if I were a poet I would go on and say: dust to dust but may the clean morning air still blow across the sky."

Marguerite recited one more quatrain

Ye heavens! From this day my eye will make so bold
The azure vault's glittering diamonds to behold.
I willingly deny idols who did not roam
The palatial halls spanned by its rolling dome.

Her husband listened with the blissful admiration of the well-heeled peasant. The canon who was aware that she hadn't learned rhymed couplets upstream of the Rivière des Envies believed he understood what she was referring to. He later asked her to recite some more. She answered that poetry had died out, meaning that her relationship with Armour Lupien hadn't just been a physical one.

"Mrs. Cossette, there is something I still can't figure out. He was no longer here when he worked on his Laval university literature course and went into raptures over Rotrou's plays."

"Philippe can tell you. We got letters from Saint-Thuribe where his favourite verses had been copied down. There were no comments."

In the presbytery, Florence, Canon Tourigny's housekeeper, wasn't happy at all. She was nursing a mood of gloomy resignation which couldn't quite conceal bad temper and which the maids as well as the sexton and even the new assistant shared. One day, during dinner, the canon reminded his curate that one of the duties of a parish priest was to give a grounding in Latin to children who had a natural turn for it and whose fathers could consider shouldering the costs of a seminary education. After the meal he went to smoke a cigar at the house of Philippe and Marguerite Cossette, the cigar he'd been smoking at home for so long, whose aroma Florence had grown used to, to the point where she couldn't do without it. As she ate while clearing the table, the young assistant repeated to her that a parish priest should teach Latin to a boy of well-to-do parents. She laughed at him.

"Teach Latin to little Mithridates? There's a piece of news for you. It's obvious you don't know his mother. She's from up north. My late father who used to farm, out in Sainte-Geneviève, wouldn't even have wanted her for a charwoman. You haven't seen her? With those glittering eyes. The woman's an Injun!''

''Miss Florence, at the seminary they didn't teach me to discriminate between one race and another.''

''An Injun woman ain't no race, she's a girl just good enough to pick mushrooms, who'd rather have black currants than religion and won't ever agree to have her son taken away from her.''

''She's still a good mother.''

''You call that a good mother? She'll make a bum out of that fine little boy. He'll be getting into brawls and chasing girls. Anyone who wants to teach him Latin is nuts.''

She stopped speaking, overcome with emotion, tears streaming down her cheeks.

''The truth is Canon Tourigny never got over Dr. Fauteux's death. He goes to Mithridates' home because the doctor used to. The poor man of God! I don't know if they taught you to pray or to be a politician in Trois-Rivières, but if they taught you to pray think about Canon Tourigny. He's been having a hard time and it makes everyone in the presbytery miserable. It's never happened before. It's awful. Go pray to our Lord, you poor man. You couldn't do anything better.''

The assistant didn't leave the table. He sat there, thinking. He was an intelligent young man and thanked God for the gift of faith as well as for having made him His priest.

''You have been generous in all things except age. You number my days by the dropful as if You, whose name is the Eternal, weren't in possession of age and time.''

To whom could he appeal so as to express his doubts and his dissatisfaction? Since he was beginning to feel sleepy and fought it off at the risk of a headache, he thought of the crown of thorns. He should appeal to the Son made incarnate in space and crucified in time. It was a revelation to him. He went up to bed and, after a while, when he was dozing off, heard Canon Tourigny coming in.

The loss of his wife had attracted Dr. Fauteux to the Mithridates' large residence near the bridge. The loss of his friend certainly influenced the canon's advances but, above all, his feelings towards the young boy did it, the child he had brought back from the cemetery, who had unsettled him, the boy named Armour whom he had until then refused to see, the son of the best-loved of his assistants. If he could appreciate the qualities and virtues of the boy's mother besides it was because he loved horses first and was a canon and a man of God second. As to Philippe, the legitimate father, the owner of the toll-bridge, *The Saint Elias,* as well as of two schooners, he also was one of the village's most prosperous farmers. He had made even more of a pile since his marriage and several families depended on this fortune. He was prone to watch over the development of the parish because of it, which made him a man to be reckoned with as far as the canon was concerned.

"Philippe, did you notice that our cemetery has attracted as many people as a small place of pilgrimage would for some time now?"

"Yes, and I can even prove it to you, thanks to the returns from the bridge. Are you expecting any miracles?"

"No. I'd expect a reprimand on the whole. All these visitors seem interested in what's behind the Calvary."

"A Senegalese idol, Father Tourigny. A fairly

rare thing in these parts."

"They might not appreciate this rarity in the episcopal palace. Tell me Philippe, it isn't carved out of ebony, is it? I have the impression it was made out of soft-wood and shouldn't last too long."

"It certainly seemed unusually light to all of my sailors. Captain Maheu even claims that to preserve it, it should be put into a glass alcove like the big statue of Sainte-Anne in Machiche."

"We may not build an alcove for it but it'll stand where we put it as long as it lasts, no matter what His Excellency thinks. And wouldn't you know, I'm expecting his visit."

"For the reprimand?"

"Yes."

"Philippe Cossette, there's one little favour I'd ask of you. When the bishop comes up to the bridge's toll-gate make him pay like everyone else does."

"Canon, do you think I can afford to let as large a carriage as the bishop's go by on my bridge free of charge?"

"You can afford even less to let it come up to the gate at a fast trot. Don't forget that your bridge is less solid than you might think, that trotting on it is forbidden and that offenders must pay a fine. Make sure you collect both the toll and the fine."

"I'll watch over my interests. For my part, could I suggest that you padlock the cemetery gate? I believe I saw several of the pilgrims blasphemously driving into the place."

His Excellency Charles-Olivier came instead of Bishop Laflèche. His carriage drove across the bridge, at a walk, up to the gate. The toll collector came out. Bishop Caron asked to pass free of charge as was customary for ecclesiastics. The toll collector answered that no one knew anything about ecclesiastics on Batiscan's bridge and that the gate was only opened to citizens who had paid their toll. The apostolic protonotary threatened him with Canon Tourigny's anathema. The man laughed at him and His Excellency understood that there was something new here. He had no inclination for chicanery and simply headed back for Trois-Rivières.But on the following morning the carriage came back at a fast trot, bringing the bishop himself in a temper, not asking to pass free of charge but demanding it in the name of Church authority. Philippe who had expected this return and this anger stood at the gate himself.

"His Excellency is riding high this morning. He forgets that before he can talk about tolls he must pay a fine for trotting up to the gate."

"Trotting up? Fiddlesticks!"

"Driver, did you or didn't you come at a trot? Tell me and I'll take your word for it."

Bishop Laflèche leaning out of the carriage-door was nonplussed. He couldn't believe his ears when he heard his coachman answer Philippe Cossette:

"I've got to admit that I couldn't slow my horses down, Mr. Cossette, and they did trot on the bridge."

"Your Excellency, you owe me a five dollar fine unless you care to contradict your coachman and lie before God."

Bishop Laflèche pulled a five dollar bill out of his purse and threw it up in the air. An unexpected gust of wind blew it into the river.

"Department of Transport regulations are formal. The fine must be paid to the owner of the toll-bridge and not to the river. Your Excellency may dive in and bring back this first bill or be so good as to hand me a second.''

As Philippe Cossette was speaking, the sailors of *The Saint Elias* who looked determined were closing in. Some were huge chaps, very impressive. Bishop Laflèche pulled another bill out of his purse, handed it to his coachman who gave it to Philippe Cossette, very politely.

''Lovely,'' he said, ''all we have to do now is have the justice of the peace come over so he can report on the incident to the satisfaction of both parties.''

''You're not suggesting...''

''I will have Your Excellency know the law stipulates that such a report should be made for your own protection, not mine. I've already got your five dollars. You'll have the report, provided you pay for the costs, which goes without saying.''

''I don't need it. Raise that gate and let me pass.''

Philippe Cossette asked Bishop Laflèche whether he intended to return to Trois-Rivières the same day.

''Do you imagine that I would spend the night here after the outrage which has just been committed against me?''

''Then, it'll be a crown for a two-way crossing.''

''What? The religious authorities have never been subject to paying the toll.''

One of the sailors cut in to say that if Jesus had walked on the waters, His Excellency must have learned to outdo him since, and that every man in the village would be delighted to know that he had crossed the river in his carriage, horses and all, without using the bridge.

''It would be a great miracle.''

109

Philippe Cossette held out his hand.

"One crown or a miracle."

His Excellency took a crown out of his purse and handed it to the owner of the bridge.

"It's a crown I shall remember."

"We know just what Your Excellency means. With a little more faith you could have crossed the river free of charge."

When the gate was opened the episcopal carriage started off at a smart trot, not towards the presbytery, as might have been expected, but towards the cemetery's fence whose entrance gate had just been padlocked.

"If I'd known," Philippe Cossette said, "I'd have let him through for nothing. It isn't every day you see a bishop making a pilgrimage to the potter's field to pay his respects to a big, flat-faced idol with stark-naked tits."

At the cemetery gate, His Excellency was losing patience.

"Go and get the key at the presbytery."

The coachman ran over. The housekeeper told him to address himself to the churchwarden.

"You're in luck. He's just left for Trois-Rivières. So he's going your way, isn't he."

The coachman had the definite impression that not only would his bishop not meet with good will in Batiscan but that he had gotten into a mess. He returned to tell the bishop the answer he had been given which indeed seemed to imply that he was expected to go back where he came from.

"Well, nothing keeps us from going on foot to have a look at this notorious idol."

"Do you want me to go with Your Excellency?"

"No. Take care of the horses. Things being what

they are somebody might help them break loose. I'm not suspicious by nature but I don't feel I can trust these people."

"Mixed feelings, like when you were with the Sioux?"

"My poor man, the Sioux were Magouas and Gypsies compared to these members of my diocese. A man like Philippe Cossette, especially if he's acting in collusion with Canon Tourigny would be capable of selling me as a slave to the niggers. He is impudent enough and powerful enough to do it too. It isn't that pleasant for a bishop who is reputedly an autocrat to feel he has no authority and that he's stirred up a hornet's nest."

Bishop Laflèche entered the cemetery and walking round the Calvary scene made his way directly to the potter's field. Some particulars of the idol reminded him of certain tall totem poles he had seen in the Canadian West. After all, except for the bare breasts he'd found nothing to say against it. It was hideous, it would scare the kids off and stood exactly where it should. He walked back to his carriage, thoughtful, even wondering whether the breasts could be considered scandalous.

"Well?" his coachman asked.

"I believe," His Excellency said, "that it would have been more polite of me to call on Canon Elias Tourigny to begin with."

"Should I take Your Excellency to the presbytery?"

"You'll have to, my dear man."

Once at the presbytery, Bishop Laflèche wasn't at all sure of himself: what if the canon refused to welcome him?

"My dear man, go and inquire. He might not be in."

He wasn't.

"You'll find him at Mr. Philippe Cossette's."

His Excellency hesitated.

"Are you afraid of being sold as a slave to the niggers in Africa?"

"If I didn't stop over it would indeed seem that I was. And I'm thinking of you, my dear man. Were I to be sold into slavery, with a ring hanging from my nose, you'd be coming along. And just look at how fat you are. Why, you'd sail across the ocean only to be dumped into a huge cauldron... All things considered, we will stop over. Besides, it would be unthinkable for a bishop to come snooping about a parish without giving his regards to the pastor."

"God speaks through Your Excellency's mouth."

"Does he, my dear man?"

"He's anxious to see us back in Trois-Rivières and the best way of doing it is to go and say hello to the canon as well as to King Mithridates who can allow us to cross the bridge or stop us. The Romans protect you in Trois-Rivières. No matter how I listen I haven't heard anyone speaking English here."

The bishop's carriage stopped before Philippe Cossette's home. His Excellency darted out even before the coachman had gotten off his bench.

"You wait for me here. Unhitching the horses for any reason whatsoever is out of the question. We're only dropping in and I'll be out in a minute. What's more, you may know that His Holiness doesn't need the protection of the Romans."

From the outside, the King's home didn't look like much. It was an old French house. A wing which harmonized rather well with it had been added. As he came in, Bishop Laflèche was astonished: the whole house, from one fireplace to another and from the

112

floor to the ceiling had been converted into a living-room. Strangely enough, a seemingly useless rope hung from one of the two beams. His Excellency had no time to notice it. He only realized that he was faced by forty men, Philippe Cossette's sailor boys and Canon Elias Tourigny's churchwardens. This show of strength occupied both ends of the living-room while the middle remained vacant. Facing the entrance, along the opposite wall, Captain Maheu, the first churchwarden, Marguerite and Philippe Cossette sat in several large wicker-chairs. Canon Elias Tourigny was sitting in the biggest one. A smaller chair wasn't taken. None of these people seemed to have noticed the arrival of Bishop Laflè-che who now felt much less brisk than when he had stepped out of the carriage. With his hooked nose and keen eyes he gave the impression of being a bird of prey caught in a trap. He turned round and saw that the door was blocked by half a dozen men who were much bigger than his driver. Rock solid. The sailor who had insulted him at the toll-gate stood among them.

Bishop Laflèche was high-strung by temperament, well known for his impetuousness and his wrath, inclined to panic.

"I'll bet I'm going to be captured," he thought, "and thrown into the ship's hold. They'll go and trade me off, me, the representative of His Holiness, as a slave in Africa."

He was bewildered, obsessed by this ridiculous idea. He didn't notice a young boy delivering an address to him and from panic, the high-strung prel-ate went to ecstasy, wondering where such a very pretty voice could come from.

"Oh! It's you my child! And whatever *do you*

have to tell me?''

Armour Cossette wasn't embarrassed. He let the greetings he had memorized be, and answered His Excellency:

''Sir, because I am the youngest, I came to greet the greatest man here and ask him to bless me. Everyone will be blessed as well when I'll have been blessed by you.''

''I will be very pleased to do it, young man. Very pleased indeed.''

Armour Cossette kneeled and Bishop Laflèche blessed him three times, while the sailors and churchwardens stood there and the Canon, Marguerite, Philippe Cossette, the captain of *The Saint Elias* as well as the first churchwarden remained seated. Then the little boy took His Excellency by the hand and brought him to his seat between Marguerite Cossette and Canon Tourigny, a wicker chair smaller than the one occupied by the *curé* of Batiscan.

''Your Excellency,'' Marguerite said, holding his hand,'' we will never forget what you have just done for us.''

And she kissed his hand as women like her, women with fiery, almond-shaped eyes, women of the American Indian nations out West had done when he had brought them the word of God while their livestock, the huge herd of wild buffalo, was being exterminated.

''This nice little boy is yours?''

''Yes, Your Excellency.''

''I would have thought so. On account of his eyes.''

Canon Tourigny asked:

''Is it true that Mrs. Duplessis, the distinguished wife of the honorable Nérée is in an interesting condition again but that she's expecting a boy this time?''

114

Bishop Laflèche eyed Canon Tourigny with a thoughtful look. If Judge Duplessis' residence wasn't far from the episcopal palace, the famous Honoré Mercier had also been paying questionable visits to her.[1] It was certainly a shrewd as well as a troubling query.

"So I have heard," he answered.

He couldn't help admiring the old man's subtle mind. In Batiscan it invested him with an authority beside which his own was negligible even though he was the canon's bishop.

"Tell me, Father Tourigny, does Batiscan look like a bigger town than Trois-Rivières to you?"

"Trois-Rivières looks bigger but one shouldn't forget that outsiders are very influential there while here, they're not."

Champagne was being served. Canon Tourigny added.

"We've broken out of the Gulf and we're trading with several nations. That's how we can drink champagne while you're mostly drinking rotgut. You're sitting there, crushed under your own weight. You can escape to nowhere else but Rome and believe me, Your Excellency, it's just a safety valve, the safety valve of illusion because Vatican diplomacy can only get on well with the British diplomatic corps."

The first churchwarden had begun to speak.

"May I propose a toast to the health of His Excellency who has touched the heart of everyone in Batiscan by coming to pray at the grave of Dr. Fauteux. The doctor is a man whose death we still

---

[1] According to local rumor, Maurice Duplessis, the late premier of Quebec, was the illegitimate child of Bishop Laflèche or Honoré Mercier.

mourn. He now lies with the insane and the unfortunate in the potter's field.''

Everyone drank his glass down, slowly, and Bishop Laflèche answered:

''My children, I'm not sorry I came here although my visit wasn't an official one. If it had been I would have called on your parish priest first. Today, I understood why Christ, when taking upon himself the sins of the world had jeopardized his reputation at the time. I have seen the goddess of death and its horror which had been denounced to me as scandalous. I am not certain that it is. In any case it was sculptured out of light and brittle wood and the muckrakers who often cry shame because the disgrace is in themselves will simply have to wait. Your bishop will no longer listen to them. He leaves it to the verdict of time.''

Canon Tourigny then said in reply:

''You know that I am a man of peace. Let me tell you that in a few words you have reconciled me to my bishop. I should hope that he is aware of this and will count on me whenever he works for peace.''

The glasses had been filled. This time it was Philippe Cossette who asked all present to drink to a long life for *The Saint Elias*.

''Philippe you rascal, you're talking parish-pump politics!'' yelled the sailor who had insulted His Excellency on the bridge.

''This is my parish. The ship I was talking about bears the name of a man we all love. It's the name of my country which is out there wherever outsiders haven't got it licked. We're free here, we have the initiative. We're not under anybody's thumb, we're men. We've been locked in, but a country isn't a jail. It's like a big get-together where you learn to mix with people from all over. Thanks to that windjammer,

116

the craftsmanship of the carpenters, the guts of the crew and the skill of the captain we've broken out of this land and we've gotten in touch again with the big wide world. And who the hell are we? Country people. But we've travelled farther than the city boys of Trois-Rivières, Montreal and Quebec who've got foreigners lording it over them and are expecting these guys to do things they should be doing for themselves. My friends, I drink to *The Saint Elias,* I drink to my country's freedom, I drink to the whole wide world.''

Of all the people present, the bishop of Trois-Rivières was the most affected. When he crossed the bridge again, the gate was up and the toll-collector touched his cap to him politely.

"My good man, do you know what?'' said Bishop Laflèche to his coachman. ''I raise my voice and everyone in this country hears me. But I haven't got anything like the authority and the power of Canon Tourigny.''

CHAPTER 10

The Saint Elias whose figurehead was an angel, its wings spread out and swept back against the ship's bow, was sailing downriver, going by the Notre-Dame mountains up to Pointe-à-la-Frégate and from there into the Gulf up to the southern straits between Newfoundland and Cape Breton Island. Then it travelled towards Bermuda or the West Indies with a cargo of pine lumber which Captain Maheu bartered as best he could and whenever he could, from one year to the next. He only made three crossings to Africa and the old country. Pine hadn't cost much at the beginning of the great devastation of the Laurentians. Then the price went up and you couldn't find any, while at the same time sailing ships found themselves outdistanced by steamers. If it hadn't been for Captain Maheu's lifelong habit of sailing for the islands, the angel of *The Saint Elias* might have beaten its wings in vain and the ship would have remained at the mouth of the Batiscan.

"Captain Maheu, you have to keep on sailing even if you only do it for the sake of Marguerite and the canon."

"Mithridates, you're not even getting a return on your investment," the captain answered Philippe Cossette who was squandering whatever he earned with two stinking little schooners.

"I know we're not going to have any more good years but I've gotten used to the sheer beauty of seeing you come back home. The sails of *The Saint Elias* can be seen as far off as Sainte-Anne."

"Especially when it takes me over a week to come up from Grondines."

"You're coming in against more of a wind now there aren't any more pines, but that's no reason to quit. Besides, there wouldn't be a market for a ship which was built meticulously and according to what amounts to a lost art."

The canon had been able to get the better of his bishop — and local rumor would still have it that as His Excellency travelled back to Trois-Rivières he'd annulled the blessings bestowed on the cows and pigs by Father Normand who had mistaken them for the future members of his diocese — but in the long run, the canon couldn't put up with the increasingly dim-witted and hysterical assistants whom the seminary churned out for him.

"Good God!" he'd say, "I'll end up hating my own people."

After the death of Bishop Caron, he asked permission to go and choose a successor for himself since he no longer felt he had the nerve or the strength to train priests for other parishes. This is how he lived on into old age with Father Rondeau who was later to become the pastor of Sainte-Catherine, near Quebec, after a quarrel with Bishop Cloutier who was admittedly touched in the head but less delirious than Archbishop Paul Bruchési. The apostolic delegates of our Holy Father the Pope — the latter had become infallible in 1870 — still thought the world of Bishop

120

Cloutier but they were never more than pompous flunkeys, or by turn dangerous conspirators, filthy rich and rotten to the core. Such was the case with Monsignor Antoniotti who came to Ottawa from Madrid after General Franco's coup. The man was exclusively answerable to Pius XII who couldn't implement policy without hitting below the belt, good and hard, rendering thanks to God for atrocities and little birds. Bishop Roche as well as a Roman Countess, Mrs. Rivest, née Berthiaume, were his close acquaintances. And this sinister Pope who was famous for countless follies, particularly the fresco to the right of the main altar in the old Notre-Dame de Bonsecours Church showing him enraptured before an apparition of the Virgin, compelled Canadian religious orders to be governed from Rome since he wanted to set them up as a sinecure.

Towards the end of his life, Canon Tourigny was apprehensive of the future, since he was a member of a national Church which was to become disillusioned with the papacy. He went to pray at the grave of the doctor once a month and asked his friend who had been an agnostic to help him keep faith. As the years went by, he could assess the damage inflicted by them on the big Senegalese idol which was crumbling. It had lost its teeth, one ear, and its face seemed flatter than ever. Only the breasts whose nipples were as large as a cow's dugs held out. It certainly didn't look nicer, but there was no longer anything hideous or repulsive about it. ''My poor friend. What's become of you under the earth? I still remember you because you're lying among the forsaken and the insane. As you became their protector you may have remained un-touched by corruption and may now be younger than I am.''

One day, Marguerite asked the old canon to hear her confession.

"I would certainly want to, my dear girl, but I don't even know who you are. I know where you come from and I'm not unaware of two things. One is that you were first considered an intruder here because you had snatched the parish's best match away from a number of vintage families who had girls they wanted to marry off. The second is that you didn't ruin him as people hoped you would. On the contrary, you urged him on and made him a much richer man."

"I can't take the credit. Dr. Fauteux was his adviser."

"Yes, possibly, but didn't he become rich because, as he had no prejudices, he wanted everyone to know what you were worth?"

"I wasn't worth much, Father. I just liked fancy talk and I could remember some poems I never read. I learned them by rote."

"Yes, but just who are you?"

Marguerite lowered her head to think. The canon saw her counting on her fingers. Then she looked up and said that her ancestors belonged to five or six ethnic groups.

"My paternal grandfather whose name was Trépanier was Abenaki. He switched his name to Trépanier out of friendship, that's sure, but there are two different versions of just what happened. The first says he came from Bécancourt and his hunting grounds lay along the Rivière des Envies but, I like the second better: a man called Trépanier was working as a foreman for this Mr. Sénécal who specialized in laying railroad tracks and then going bankrupt so the railroad could be bought up by a London businessman who'd get it cheap. He was nominated to the Senate in return for his services just as his colleague, Forget, became a Lord and his wife a Lady. It's true that Forget had been swindling mostly the French while Sénécal would swindle anybody. They say he even took an Englishman called Samuel Butler for a sucker and Butler wrote a book called *Erewhon* where these people live happily ever after because they keep the machinery they've invented but which they're smart enough not to use in a museum. The book was probably written in Montreal too.''

''Girl, you're a walking, talking encyclopedia.''

''I just listened in on a couple of scholars. In bed, mostly. Anyhow, after Sénécal had built the railroad which goes from Quebec to Montreal and on to Ottawa, he thought he was going too straight. So, right after, he starts laying tracks from Lévis to the Kenebec River. When they stretched beyond Sertignan, Trépanier who was one of his foremen saw an Indian with his hair plaited who seemed upset about this bunch of madmen in his hunting grounds and wondering whether they came to make war. Well, Trépanier walked up to him nice and friendly like, took out his canteen and drank up. He wiped the neck of the bottle with his sleeve and offered it to the Indian who took a gulp and thanked him. They were friends before they'd even said a word. From then on they were never out of each other's sight. When Trépanier died, the Abenaki simply assumed his name and took care of his widow who gave him several more children called Trépanier like the others.

''Your father was one of the youngest?''

''Yes. Another thing is that on my mother's side — her name was Pagnol — …''

''Marchand or Massicotte?'' asked the canon.

''I couldn't tell you, Father… On my mother's side

123

I'm Irish, Montagnais and *Tête de boule*. That's four. They say I'm also related to Lord Hamelin's Indian girls in Grondines. He used to go and get them in Missouri.''

"That's five. You must also be a *Canadienne*. Of course, since your mother's name was Pagnol.''

"Well, that's who I am, Father.'' Marguerite Cossette said.

"An unlikely miss. Who would have thought you'd become the first lady of Batiscan?''

When the canon heard her cool-headed answer he couldn't believe it.

"I was always absolutely sure I would.''

This self-confidence accounted for the ease with which Marguerite had maintained her status as well as the extent to which she had influenced her husband. It also accounted for her individualism, the liberties she had taken with the existent mores and even, perhaps, religion.

"Are you a Christian, at least?''

"Father, I'll admit I hadn't thought about it much up to now. Dr. Fauteux had told me that if I wasn't going to be discriminated against because of my origins, I couldn't afford not to be seen in church and I had to attend on Sundays and feast-days, go to the altar rail with my husband on great occasions, especially when the Mithridates family ran the risk of being penalized or reprimanded for one reason or another.''

"My girl, I'm sure that both your husband and you have put on quite a show but I'm still uncertain about one thing: I shut my eyes in the shadow of the confessional and I don't hear your voice on the other side of the shutter. Did you ever go to confession?''

"I trusted my husband all the way and considered

124

his confession mine.''

"Marguerite, when you were cheating..."

"The devil knew it and there was no need of disturbing God."

The canon nodded.

"God," he said, "God."

He felt that he was in the presence of a genuine pagan.

"Why do we even send missionaries to the Zulus and shut the whores of Gabon up in convents?"

"I beg your pardon?"

"I was talking to myself — a slip of the tongue — I am old, Marguerite, very old. Each month, I see a piece falling off the idol in the potter's field. I think it looks more beautiful and more wretched. I look up at it without feeling scared at all, which means that the goddess of death must be creeping up on me."

"The breasts are still on it."

"Well, what am I supposed to do, stand there and be outraged? It began a long, long time ago, farther back than I can remember. Far from terrifying me, its breasts quench the thirst of my anguish."

Marguerite Cossette, the mother of Mithridates II thanks to Father Armour Lupien, had to remind Canon Tourigny that she had come to confess her sins, but the old man wouldn't even hear of it.

"Have you at least been baptized?"

This time her answer was harsh:

"You're a municipal magistrate in charge of register first and a pastor second."

"What do you know. I heard that somewhere before from a man who was trying to let me have it but who still sounded like a friend. It is true that I'm in charge of the registers of births, marriages and

125

deaths. If I put you down as Marguerite Trépanier, you are Marguerite Trépanier, not Babalou or Portenqueue."

The poor man was talking wildly.

"Listen to me, Canon Tourigny."

"I have, girl. I've heard it all. May God forgive you. Go and sin no more."

"I mean, listen to all the sins I've committed."

"I'm too old. I wouldn't have the time. It's too late. I have given you absolution and I can't take it back. As a penance, keep on being proud, and straightforward, and as good as you can be, because God wouldn't be God if he required more from you."

The following morning, the canon went to pray at the grave of Dr. Fauteux and returned to the presbytery feeling thirsty. Satan or one of Bishop Laflèche's more devoted followers had dared to stand up to him and sawed off both the idol's breasts. He had Philippe Cossette come over and said to him:

"I have lost the milk of my childhood, which means that my life is coming to an end. You will have the idol taken away today. It was defaced by a fanatic last night. Burn it at the mouth of the Batiscan River, near the St. Lawrence, beside the church. In our parish, beauty and strength will spring up from its ashes. Philippe, you were nicknamed Mithridates and I ratify the existence of your dynasty. May little Armour become Mithridates II and see your wealth grow…"

The canon found it difficult to speak. Cossette opened his mouth to answer him but Father Tourigny motioned him to be silent. Florence, her face distorted by tears, went to fetch Father Rondeau. The assistant who was waiting in the kitchen came to read the handwritten will of his pastor which stip-

126

ulated that he would inherit all of the canon's personal property provided he took charge of his old servants and dealt with them as he would with relatives. A rather considerable sum in cash went with the property.

"So," Canon Tourigny said, "my successor, pastor Rondeau, will not be harassed by the episcopal palace... Go on, Father."

The balance of the liquid assets, which Philippe Cossette hadn't thought so considerable, went to the latter on one condition: that *The Saint Elias* would sail for one year more, even if the forests were totally depleted and the saw-mills were closing down for lack of pine lumber.

"Let it go on principle, for the sheer beauty of it, so that the ship can return home one last time, its sails spread out."

This is how the man who liked horses sacrificed the interests of his next of kin to water which surrounds the continents; water which belongs to all and to no one, which both separates and joins the nations. He declared himself the citizen of a free country, the kingdom of Mithridates, hostile to the Romans, a land where it felt good to be a fellow-countryman and to speak the same language, to be united by a kinship transcending all others; and he declared himself a citizen of the world as well. His will ended with the words: "Glory and beauty are patient; when they have seen the light of day they bide their time because the future belongs to them."

The Saint Elias had just weighed anchor when the parish priest was on the point of death. He called out "I am thirsty," over and over again. His servants didn't know how to comfort him, especially Florence who had stopped drinking. At least she would suffer from thirst as he did. Marguerite Cossette, her husband Philippe and Armour her son who was going to be fifteen, dropped in during the evening. The young boy looked like Father Lupien to the point where he was growing into the living image of his sacrilege. The dying man stopped moaning and wispered:

"Thank you, my Lord, for having given me back a mother's breasts as well as the milk of my early childhood. I have been a man. Now, I will become the whole universe."

Father Rondeau recited the prayers for the dead slowly, serenely. So died Canon Elias Tourigny — the beloved pastor of Batiscan and the oldest canon of the Trois-Rivières diocese.

CHAPTER 11

After it had returned from its last crossing which
was a foolish and expensive venture, the late canon's
quiet tribute to Marguerite, to his parish and to his
country, *The Saint Elias* ran aground and was
stranded in a slimy cove off the Batiscan. Some time
later, the kingdom of Mithridates, which continued to
wax from one defeat to another moved to the county
of Maskinongé. It did so because of the lady of The
Six Nations who cared less for wealth than for the
beauty of things. The dereliction of the sailing ship
which was still sound and sturdy, the only three-
master ever built in the village, unequalled from Sorel
to the Island of Orléans, had humiliated her. She remembered that her husband wasn't the father of her
son. A good farm, two schooners, one toll-bridge
didn't impress her since there would be other farms,
schooners and bridges but there was only one *Saint
Elias* whose amazing runs filled her with pride. No
matter how Philippe Cossette asserted that Captain
Maheu had died of yellow fever in King Christophe's
Cape Haiti castle she wouldn't believe it; he had lost
her respect. And yet, Marguerite the daughter of six
nations and of a family of nobodies from beyond the
Rivière des Envies should have been his humble ser-

vant. In Batiscan, the Cossettes had been held in high esteem since the beginning, on a par with the Desilets, the Marchands, the Barils, and the Massicottes, at least. Philippe had kept his fine farm, his bridge, his schooners as well as some cash which made him an eminent man, a man of property, if not a king, but he remained his wife's vassal. The studied contempt, which he felt subject to, and which dogged his steps wherever he went, affected him so deeply that he died before his time. Whereupon, Marguerite who preferred beauty to a profit contrived to outmanoeuver greed. Advised by Father Rondeau, she sold her land, her schooners and her bridge for more than they were worth. She already had a first mortgage on the house of Dr. Hamelin in Louiseville; "a house with five doors," said the doctor's wife who was a silly and conceited woman. The doctor who wasn't called on except to sign death certificates and treat sore throats had three sons. While they didn't seem all that prodigal with money, they were gradually ruining him, in fact. The farmer from Chacoura who took a second mortgage on the house was a fool, especially as his name was Lesage. He only got the interest during the first three years. Then he didn't get a cent and lost his capital. Money was getting scarce when the poor doctor died and the house which was put up for sale wasn't even worth the price of the first mortgage. Marguerite moved in. She had been smart enough to sell the farm as well as the bridge while keeping the house which adjoined both. Father Rondeau had circulated the rumor that she preferred beauty to affluence, and that she was seduced into some very bad investments out of sheer extravagance; this also accounted for her fifteen year old son's staying at home without any kind of education.

"Are you considering his own best interests when you keep him at home?"

"Father Rondeau, tell anyone who's nosey enough to ask that I'm going bankrupt."

"I can't go around telling that kind of yarn. Montreal Scotchmen are the only people richer than you are."

"Do it for chastity's sake. I can't say no to a man. You should be aware of that."

The priest blushed. He thought she was trying to tell him something, especially as Marguerite seemed to have turned devout of late. Each week she confessed the sexual fantasies which were taboo for a good Christian. He advised her to go to communion every day. She would go on the first day and then give it up. Father Rondeau, in spite of the divine grace bestowed upon him by the priesthood was still a conceited man by nature. Instead of telling her that she didn't have a thing to worry about, he objected to her son's presence at home whenever, alas, he gave in to temptation and came to visit her. Now Marguerite was very fond of her son and she would rather have him ignorant than miserable and riddled with pimples at the Trois-Rivières seminary.

"When he's old enough, *Monsieur le curé*, I'll find him a girl from a good family. She'll be well educated and she'll write his letters and do his bookkeeping for him."

Father Rondeau, whose first sin ever was this fine-looking widow, began to circulate the rumor that she was ruined. He did so hesitatingly at first, then with a semblance of truth, when during a visit Marguerite told him that birth certificates weren't always reliable:

"In what way?"

She simply answered that her son whose name was

Cossette was the child of the ex-pastor of Saint-Thuribe.''

"Oh! He was quite a poet! Just think of what he was referring to when he wrote:

Ye heavens! From this day my eye will make so bold
The azure vault's glittering diamonds to behold.
I shall die laughing at husbands who never roam
The palatial halls spanned by its rolling dome
For now, my hand hath plucked the finest fruits of
love
As glorious a splendor as the stars above.

Meanwhile she had bought the house in Louiseville. The owner of the farm and the bridge rushed over to offer her a modest price for her residence. He was sure of getting it but she only laughed at him.

"You won't be able to keep both of them up, madame.''

"Mr. Massicotte,'' she said, "I am definitely moving to Louiseville, but you shouldn't have believed groundless rumors and hoped to get your hands on a house you want for a song.

"I'm offering you a reasonable price.''

She showed him her account books.

"I want twice as much or the house will be converted into a hotel.''

She got the price she had asked and Mithridates' kingdom moved from Batiscan to the county of Maskinongé. Father Rondeau, who was no fool and demonstrated the fact in Sainte-Catherine near Quebec, told Marguerite who was listening to him, tongue in cheek:

"I thank God for having met one bright girl. She'll protect me from the others.''

"Since I'll be leaving, Father, allow me to show

132

you around the house.''

He obtained the favors he'd been dreaming of. When they came back down, he said:

''Madame, I don't understand. One tends to go from contradiction to contradiction with you. Do you love me?''

''Not at all,'' Marguerite answered laughing.

''Then, why did you...?''

''Why? Let's say that if you leave a man unsatisfied, it's bad for his health. There's nothing wrong in giving him what he wants, either.''

Father Rondeau went on:

''If I ever went to visit you in Louiseville...''

''You would be told that you don't have to be thanked twice. Let's part like friends, shall we?''

He left her like a good parish priest should and never again tried to betray God and the Virgin with another woman.

''I'm an idiot, Marguerite.'' he told her. ''I was no longer expecting anything from you and you leave me with something I'll remember to my dying day: as glorious a splendor as the stars above...''

''Father,'' she said, smiling, ''just pray for me. You weren't cut out to be a poet.''

They never had occasion to see each other again. In Sainte-Catherine, however, when Mrs. Garneau came into the confessional and he noticed her husband who was an artilleryman standing guard so that no one would hear the petty sins she had been brooding over, he thought of Marguerite, her almond-shaped eyes and cool head, so different from this fool who thought of herself as a lady and reveled in her own vacuousness. Marguerite had been his lone adventure. For a member of the clergy who isn't a homosexual, who doesn't squirm because he's obsessed by what he hasn't done and feels he's not up to doing, that is a very model of virtue. He would never again find what he had in Batiscan, but he didn't want to become less of a man for that. He spoke out, candidly, and wasn't easily intimidated — not even by the timorous ones like Mrs. Garneau to whom he always talked in a loud voice.

"What can I do," he would say, "I'm hard of hearing. The secrets of the confessional tend to echo."

The lady regretted the whispering Jesuit who was her confessor in Montreal and resorted to Father Rondeau as little as she could. It was too often at that. But he could put up with her, because she reminded him, by contrast, of his magnificent sin.

"When he is old enough," Marguerite had said. The question was how old was old enough for the son she loved and to whom she remained faithful in spite of a few brief affairs. Had the decision depended entirely on her, she would have put off the time when he was old enough for a century. Well fed, he grew into early manhood. His mother saw to it that he was denied nothing.

"I'll drink a bottle of port each time you get a new girl. You know I like port, so you can see your mother isn't standing in your way. I'll ask only two things of you. First, you should know that you're good-looking enough not to have to pay for what you get with anything but your own body... By the way, why don't you go after married women? They've got experience; outwitting another man is loads of fun, and if somebody gets pregnant, you won't find yourself with a shotgun wedding on your hands."

Canon Elias Tourigny might have been wrong when he gave her absolution without hearing her sins.

134

There's no harm in a touch of paganism when you're serving the bishop of Rome, but Marguerite was overdoing it. Had she ever been a Christian? She was very affectionate with her son and Mithridates II had gone on the prowl not so much because he liked girls but because he didn't want to be incestuous. A domineering sort, he would slap them around. He enjoyed adultery to the full, but after all, marriage is a sacrament. When he began to tire of the chase, he thought of his mother's second condition that he had forgotten to ask about. It turned out to be that he was to let her find him a wife. In the meanwhile he was making quite a reputation for himself as a mad womanizer. Money was no problem, since true to his promise, he never paid for his pleasure. One day, when he was over thirty, Marguerite suggested to him that it was time he got married.

"I've supported you up to now and you've been thrifty, which hasn't hurt you any. You'll have lots of capital to go into business with.

"How do you expect me to do that? I can barely sign my name."

"It's all settled, Armour. Your father only had Batiscan, but your kingdom is going to be the whole county of Maskinongé. You'll marry Irène Lamy. Her grandfather used to be a member of parliament. I've made a deal with him. You know the girl: she has this light, fair complexion and she's got enough education for the two of you.

"She sure is nice but I always heard she was going to become an Ursuline."

"She's going to be your wife."

"But she's not my kind of girl."

Marguerite was annoyed.

"You'll have a tug-boat and three barges to start

135

off with. Two good farmers whose barns stand out along the highway won't have to whitewash them this year. We'll paint them and anyone driving by will be able to read

ARMOUR COSSETTE, TRADER,
GRAIN AND HAY

written white over a red background. Your poor little wife is going to have a hard time doing your book-keeping and sleeping with you besides. In the southern part of Maskinongé the best families have three girls to marry off for each boy. Your offer is beyond anything Irène Lamy could expect, even if she can write well.

"I don't know a thing about hay and oats."

"You don't have to. The best is found in the Lac St. Pierre area. If you travel up and down the river-ways, you can load up near most farms and then sell the stuff going up the Ottawa River or on the Sague-nay at the big logging camps."

"I'll never be home with that kind of business."

Marguerite stroked his arm muscles.

"Come on, big boy. You're not marrying that lit-tle Ursuline to be the death of her in bed. You've been running around for fifteen years. Keep it up. You'll be doing business at the same time and she'll find a way of getting over it. You're going to be useful to each other and it's the best way for both of you to be happy."

"What about you?" he asked his mother.

He saw this woman of fifty draw herself up, her eyes as fiery as ever, her hair as abundant as in the days of her youth, her head erect. Even if it had begun to turn white, she was still wild and beautiful.

"What about me? Haven't I loved you as best I could?"

Suddenly, she felt apprehensive.

"Do you think I'm to blame for anything?"

No. He didn't. He might have been on the prowl for a long time but he'd never met a woman who was the likes of her — which is what he told her. She swelled with pride. Then, to hide how pleased she was, claimed that she felt tired.

"One's heart does get worn out. I still love you but I think I need that little Lamy girl."

Marguerite knew how to talk to him and Armour believed her. Still, if he had looked around on his wedding day as he was walking away, carefully holding the arm of a young girl whose fine, brown hair shimmered in the sunlight, he would have caught a glimpse of a woman whose mane-like hair had finally turned white, whose face was hard, beautiful, tragic. He would have seen his mother who no longer wanted to live but did not know how to die, his mother who survived out of sheer pride, who was being spoken to but not understood since she was already talking to herself. She felt she was cut out to live to be a hundred — overwhelmed by all of these unwanted years, these years of hell. What she needed was an accident, a flash of lightning, a thunderbolt she couldn't hear as she talked to herself:

"Let them cut off my breasts like they did to the idol," she said. "Let me be burned along with *The Saint Elias*, starting from the angel on its bow with its wings wide open, because I am damned! I've committed sacrilege by sleeping with a poor boy who knew a little poetry. I was itching for it but didn't care more about him than if he'd been a stud. He gave me a son and I gave the child his name. Armour will never come to any good."

She remembered her husband who had given her

137

everything she'd wanted and said:

"Get even with me, Philippe, I've double-crossed you. The son you loved so much wasn't yours. Everybody knows it. Get even with me."

And Philippe Cossette, the man she had known better than all others — even if he was a cuckold he still had been her husband — Philippe Cossette smiled away, thanked her for having resorted to every possible means of making him happy, even to cuckolding him. Much obliged! Meanwhile she didn't realize that she was crying, gently, the long-drawn tears streaming slowly down. She thought it was raining and she wasn't going to be struck by lightning because a thunderbolt which can kill you usually comes before the rain; that it was raining out of a dazzling sky when Irène Lamy's brown hair semed blond in the sunlight and her son walked away without thinking of looking back to see his mother weep... When she realized what was happening she didn't even feel embarrassed. People chatted around her but, already talking to herself she couldn't hear what they were saying. She couldn't bear it; she just didn't want to figure it all out any more, this lady of The Six Nations who never had been astonished by anything, even by her own incomprehension. She was surprised that not being able to understand, not being struck down, not having one's wings and breasts cut off could be so unendurable now. Barbaric idol. Angel of *The Saint Elias*. It was intolerable, but she would live on to be a hundred. She wept on a glorious day, amazed to have looked for an accident she no longer hoped would occur. She didn't really want to upset her son and the little Lamy girl who would see enough unhappiness without her contrivance. It was more than she could bear. She wept quietly over them, over this world which wasn't her oyster after all even if she was the lady of The Six Nations. She began to smile as she cried. While about her people had stopped talking, hands were held out and she was being congratulated.

CHAPTER 12

One can't edge backwards into life, because time moves inexorably in one direction: from the past, through the present and on into the future. Under the hands of a clock, one becomes like the dumb brutes who too are short of memory. Thus, Marguerite was growing into a very old woman who lived alone in a cottage on the other side of Rivière-du-Loup like a shrewd, silent bird in a wooden cage. When her grandson came to visit her it seemed to him that she lived on in a mythical country of the past, an imaginary land lying on the other side of the hill, a land like that of her master, Samuel Butler, who had been compelled to live in Montreal — the whore of the railroad at the time, now the whore of parking lots, gas fumes and sulphur dioxide — *Erewhon*. This grandson looked exactly like his natural grandfather and thought he took after his mother, Irène Lamy, because he had inherited the ready pen with which she'd recorded in fat account books the quantity of oats and the number of haystacks her husband had bought and sold between the two world wars.

"When I come to see you," he would tell his grandmother, "I feel as if I am not doing enough, as if I could go on the other side of the hill too."

Marguerite would smile at him and say: "The wind blows and if you don't catch it, it's gone. If you did go beyond the hills, you could set out again on *The Saint Elias*."

He would smile at her, wondering sometimes whether her mind wasn't slipping. He didn't even know of the existence of *The Saint Elias*. On the other hand, he did know the nickname he had inherited from his legitimate grandfather, although he wasn't aware of how the man had come to it, and was delighted with the kingdom which the name Mithridates III conjured up.

On this side of the hill, people still produced fire-breathing contraptions, trying to make them run faster, burning up the earth's resources as they had devastated the great timberlands which lay north of the St. Lawrence. They'd done it out of greed and made no secret of it. Now men claim they're promoting universal bliss when we're more and more aware that they're achieving just the opposite, that the pervasive, all-embracing greed produces nothing but sound and fury. Not so very long ago, some lunatics thought of themselves as supermen — a patently untenable claim. That's exactly what men are now thanks to the amount of hardware that's available. They are wrecking the planet, living on the legacy of future generations and they know that the calamity they're working towards, in the long run will occur in a matter of years if they promote their kind of industrialization everywhere. They've become supermen in fact, thanks to the squandering they call consumerism and are far more dangerous due to their lying propaganda than the so-called madmen. Because of these "supermen," a great mutation has gradually taken place which will alter all existing mythologies. Nature which used to be an omnipotent mother is becoming the daughter of all men. This may have been what Father Lupien meant when he was formulating the problem in terms of a father-son relationship:

"Verily I say unto you, it is the Son, dying on Calvary who engenders the Father and inaugurates the kingdom of God..."

At the same time, roughly, in Montreal, Butler was thinking about writing the book he was to entitle *Erewhon,* or *Over the Range*.

The son Marguerite had brought up in blissful ignorance and overprotected as long as she could before handing him over to Irène Lamy, the son she had made a fine-looking, powerful brute, lived on a grand scale. He was churning out mayors and deputies like butter pats and lumps of cheese while the *curés* danced to his tune with their cassocks tucked up, since in these blessed times when Church power was going wild, money still was the greatest of all sacraments. However, he finally ruined himself — which is inevitable when you persist in selling hay and oats in an era of tractors and gas. Moreover, his wife whose fine-spun, light chestnut-brown hair glowed in the sunlight hadn't held out against him for long. Without his records and account books, illiterate and presumptuous, he could only figure out his assets and liabilities as his temper dictated. Whiskey helped him forget his troubles, but wasn't any use as far as bankruptcy was concerned. He began to see black crosses. His brutality was beginning to turn inward. All he had to do was cross the river; his mother was expecting him. But he didn't since he had a grudge against her for having made him a baron and a barbarian. He had turned to his wife with whom he had tried to be diplomatic, although he was unable to make her happy. Now her great black cross stood where she was buried among the surrounding ones, at the feet of which ugly toads hopped about. Valerian and potassium bromide multiplied the crosses. Soon he could no longer recognize his wife's. He ran from one to the other under the gaze of a tall idol with eyes like slits, had to be put into a straightjacket and died wearing it. His son who had just received his degree as a medical practitioner, resembled his natural grandfather and practised the profession of Dr. Fauteux. He was the one who would come and visit Marguerite in her cottage on the other side of Rivière-du-Loup. He would speak to her and she would listen with a shrewd look. However, he wasn't sure she could hear what he was saying.

The kingdom of Mithridates to which a nickname had given rise had been accepted by the Cossettes as a fantasy. They had also done it because they liked to rule, because they just wouldn't speak English and couldn't stand the Romans whose stolidity seemed inept to them. Their dominion had extended from Batiscan to the county of Maskinongé and from there to the country beyond.

"Why shouldn't I be a king?" Mithridates III wondered. The third, but still the first of his own dynasty because he wasn't rich, wasn't over-equipped like an American and wrote books during his spare time. And he had decided to be one.

"I write. I create whatever I want to out of my realm. Isn't that a privilege? Everybody learns to write; to actually go ahead and do it is to use a freedom of expression akin to freedom of speech, but which few take advantage of because it's easier to talk. When you write, you write alone. Like a king."

One day, Marguerite asked him:

"What are you the king of?"

"I am the king of an uncertain country."

"Less real than Batiscan and the county of Mas-kinongé? And, will you also have a son who will reign over a great kingdom?"

Marguerite replied to her own question: his son would certainly be king of the world.

"The kingdom of Mithridates is getting larger from one defeat to the next. The world? What a disaster."

"My boy's still young. I haven't told him a thing about all of this. King of the world. After all, if he doesn't know..."

Marguerite continued:

"The poor little man could only take possession of the world and travel from one country to the other on the high seas which belong to all and to no one, if he went back to Batiscan. In a cove, near the river's mouth, there's a windjammer waiting for him; its figurehead is an angel with wings outspread. The name of the ship is *The Saint Elias*. If he doesn't do it, he won't be able to avoid disaster."